GUILTY PLEASURES

by

Cathy Yardley

MILLS & BOON®

To Liz Maverick,
one of the best writers I've ever come across,
and one of my best friends.

Kick ass, *chica!*

*First published in Great Britain 2004
by Harlequin Mills & Boon Limited,
Eton House, 18-24 Paradise Road, Richmond, Surrey TW9 1SR*

© Cathy Yardley 2002

ISBN 0 263 84045 X

14-0204

*Printed and bound in Spain
by Litografia Rosés S.A., Barcelona*

Prologue

"*What do you mean, the restaurant is closing?*"

Twenty-three-year-old Marion Worthington sat in her parents' lavish dining room. She stared down at the blue-patterned china that held the meal she was pushing around with her fork. She wasn't able to choke down a bite.

"I mean Le Pome is officially going out of business, closing up shop, going under." Marion looked up, to see her parents' horrified disbelief. "You can't honestly be surprised, after all the publicity we got."

Her mother's face was stony and impassive. "What does Derek say about all this?"

"Derek." Marion briefly looked away, fighting the tears in her eyes. Derek Black, the owner of Le Pome, the restaurant where she was the highly publicized head chef. Derek, who had been her lover up to about a month ago, when she discovered that he'd also been sleeping with the restaurant's interior decorator. She wouldn't have been surprised if it had actually been the decorator's idea to shut the place down and get young Marion Worthington out of his life forever. "It was his idea to shut us down, actually. After the disastrous reviews we had when we opened, I think he

wanted to shut us down the first month.'' Derek Black
was not a man who could handle failure, in any form.

Unfortunately, neither were the Worthingtons.

''I told you,'' her father said, looking at her mother
as if Marion herself wasn't even in the room. ''I told
you this was a stupid venture from the start. Culinary
school! For God's sake, that prepares you for *nothing*
in the real world!''

''Henry,'' her mother said warningly. Then she
turned back to Marion. ''Well. I would assume you've
learned your lesson.''

Marion nodded. She had. *Never let your parents set
you up with a ''perfect position'' with an old friend
of theirs. Never trust a bunch of old chefs and con-
sultants and marketing people rather than your own
instincts.*

Never fool yourself into thinking you're in love.

''Well, that's over with, and I for one am thankful,''
her mother said, in a business-like tone. ''You'll move
back home, of course.''

Marion looked at her, stunned. ''But, Mom…''

''And then we'll start figuring out what you're going to do next.'' Her mother's smile was crafty. ''You
know, it's a little late in the game, but I might be able
to get you on Berkeley's wait list. The dean owes me
a favor.…''

''Wait a minute,'' Marion said sharply. ''I'm not
going to college!''

Her father rolled his eyes, turning an unattractive
shade of red. ''I could have told you this was going
to happen, Claudia,'' he boomed.

Her mother's eyebrows knitted together. "Well, you're obviously not very good as a chef, Marion," her mother said, all the more hurtful in her matter-of-fact tone. "And I don't think it's a very good profession, anyway. It's unstable, it's hardly attractive…"

"Spent all that money so you could learn how to chop potatoes and carrots," her father muttered darkly. "Cooking is what uneducated people do."

Marion flushed. "I love cooking. I love *food.*"

"Well, if you love it so much, why don't you go out there and keep on cooking?" Her father stood up, a vein in his forehead pulsing. "Without your cushy restaurant, without your little helpers and hangers-on. Without Derek Black telling you what to do!"

Marion closed her eyes for a second, rage burning inside her. Something, some part of her, finally snapped. She opened her eyes.

"You were the ones that liked Derek," Marion said, her voice frozen of all emotion. "You were the ones who introduced us, who convinced him to take me on. You were the ones who liked him because he invested in Father's company."

Her mother blanched. Her father, on the other hand, stared at her with bug eyes. "I'm not saying I wasn't to blame," Marion said, feeling the pain like acid in her chest. "But damn it, I'm not going to apologize for trying. And I'm not going to be what you want me to be."

"Really? Even if it means you're going to be washing dishes and…and…I don't know what the hell else it is! Doing grunt work in some smelly, hot grease joint? How very *noble*. How completely idealistic!''

"Put it this way," Marion said, standing up and putting her napkin down on the table. "I'd rather wash dishes in a grease joint than take another bite of food from a man who has complete contempt for me.''

Her father gaped like a goldfish.

"I am so ashamed of you," her mother said in the intervening silence.

Marion spun to look at her mother, who had tears in her eyes.

"How can you talk to us like this?" Her mother's voice was muted and her eyes wide. "After all we've done for you? All the strings we've pulled? Everything we've sacrificed…''

"I never asked you to, Mother," Marion said, and earned herself another scathing glance from her father.

"Ungrateful," her father spat out. "You've never thanked us once. Well, you want to make it on your own? Don't want to ask us for anything? Then get out!''

Marion stared at them for a moment, and her mother looked away. Finally, without another word, she left.

Marion headed for her car. She sat in the driveway of the stately home on Nob Hill, the place she'd grown up in. The place she'd hated for so many years.

She was twenty-three years old. The dream of her life, her restaurant, had closed its doors forever—with enough of a cloud of failure that no one would want to hire her. Her lover had abandoned her, her family had thrown her out. She had nothing: no help, no living. No love.

She turned on the car, taking a second to brush the moisture from her eyes.

One day, I'll have a restaurant that I run my way. No more asking permission from a man who wants to use me. No more pandering to the opinions of critics. No more trying to become someone I'm not to meet the expectations of people who care more about their image and social standing than about their own daughter.

"No more," Mari whispered.

And as of that moment, she was officially starting over.

1

Seven years later

NICK AVERY STARED at the cloud-darkened sky, pulling his coat a little more tightly around him as the cold rain slapped the sidewalk in waves. It was eight o'clock at night. He'd just spent the day—hell, the past *month*—meeting with the top brass of some of the finest restaurants in San Francisco, and it had come to nothing. Now, he had just parked his car in one of the worst neighborhoods he'd been in since he was a kid, and was standing in front of a restaurant, wedged between a pawnshop and an empty storefront. The windows gleamed like a beacon of warm, welcoming light, as opposed to the shocking neon of the adult theater down the street. He glanced up at the sign: a woman, winking, her finger to her full lips in a gesture of silence.

Welcome to Guilty Pleasures.

If his mentor from the Culinary School of America hadn't specifically told him about this place, Nick thought, pushing the door open, he'd be getting back in his car by now.

The walls were painted in every color, all rich and vibrant enough to make the place explode with it. The chairs were cushioned and deep, the wine glasses un-economically large, the dishes a riot of different patterns. From the furniture to the flatware, nothing matched. If there was a style, it seemed to be Early Garage Sale. Considering the muted, tasteful décor he'd been surrounded by at Le Chapeau Noir, the restaurant he'd worked at and managed for the past four years, it was something of a shock.

It's not as much of a shock as getting fired was.

Nick gritted his teeth and walked up to the host's podium, noting how empty the restaurant seemed for a Saturday night. He wasn't going to think about Le Chapeau Noir, Phillip, or the whole ugly incident until he got this job. Then, only then, would he work on getting his reputation back.

And getting even.

A man in a tight navy T-shirt and black slacks gave Nick a once-over from the host's podium. "Table for one?"

Nick shook his head. "I'm here to see Marion Salazar."

"I see." The man smiled slyly. "Come on. Kitchen's this way."

Nick followed him to the back of the restaurant. The man pushed the swinging door that led to the kitchen opened with a flourish, and Nick was barraged by the noise and clamor of an obviously busy kitchen. "Mari! Another one!"

"Another *what*, Mo?" a female voice emerged from the ruckus.

"Applicant for the cook's job," Mo replied. At

that, the kitchen staff went quiet, staring at Nick with open curiosity. "A real yum, too," the man added. He motioned to Nick to step forward, adding in a stage whisper, "Now everybody's going to want a good look at you. Go on, work it."

Nick walked with purpose toward the back of the room. *Work it, like hell.* What had Leon sent him into, anyway?

A woman with black hair pulled back in a bun at the nape of her neck had her back to him, working over the grill, plating up what looked like meat loaf on a bed of mashed potatoes before drowning it in a savory-looking brown gravy. It smelled promising. "Order up," she said, sliding the dish into the order window with a theatric swirl. She turned to him. "So. You're applying for the cook's position, Mr....?"

He looked. No. He *gaped*.

She was wearing a black long-sleeved T-shirt instead of the requisite chef's whites, and the slogan Orgasm Donor was printed on it in bold white letters. The snug-fitting shirt molded her body like a lover's hands. She seemed poured into the jeans she was wearing, as well—and filled that container in the best possible way. Her jet-black hair, now that he was looking at her directly, sported a streak of royal purple. Her face was a perfect ivory oval, and her exotic cat-like eyes were deep violet-blue. Her lips reminded him of the full wickedness of the woman in the sign's logo. The more he stared, the more he realized that there was more than a resemblance.

She *was* the woman on the sign.

"I'm sorry, I don't know your name." Her smile was friendly, perhaps a touch flirtatious.

"Nick. Nick Avery." Mechanically, he held out a hand, trying to get his bearings. Her hand was warm in his palm. "And you'd be…Ms. Salazar?"

"Marion Salazar," she said, sending him a wink that shot an unexpected zing through his system. "Mari to my intimates."

The way she said *intimates* ought to be illegal.

Not what you're here for, Avery. He had enough problems right now. Getting lustful about his potential employer was the last thing he needed.

She glanced around the kitchen. "I know we're not terribly busy tonight," she said, her voice a low drawl, "but isn't there something else you guys could be doing?"

The crew quickly erupted into faux industry, the resulting noise almost deafening. Nick sighed. Mari smiled apologetically.

"Well, it's way too loud around here. Come on, follow me to our spare office." She pointed to a door at the back of the kitchen. It led to a little storage room with a cluttered desk in the corner. He glanced around. There were no chairs to sit on.

She perched on the desktop, letting her long legs dangle as she studied him. "So. Do you have a resumé I can look at?" She grinned. "I'm assuming you have…experience."

There it was again—that sly smile, the way that every word out of her mouth seemed to have two meanings.

He pulled his resumé out of the portfolio. She wiped a hand off on the apron tied around her hips, and took the paper, scanning it. She let out a low whistle.

"Impressive. But I don't think I can hire you."

He blinked. She couldn't have heard about what happened at Le Chapeau— Phillip wouldn't have said anything that blatant, not to someone like this. Any other restaurant owner would be afraid of a lawsuit, for potential slander, but Phillip wouldn't be—his family's flesh-eating lawyers would make him feel pretty safe there. But it had only been two weeks. Phillip had already spread the word to the four-star class restaurants in San Francisco.

Even in the restaurant community's hyper-speed grapevine, it would take longer than a few weeks to filter to an off-the-radar place like this.

"May I ask why?" he said, keeping his tone even.

"Graduated with honors from the CSA, helped open one of the most expensive and celebrated restaurants in the city, written up as one of the top ten hottest chefs in *Bon Appetit* and *Saveur* magazines?" She shook her head. "You don't want a job here."

"I wouldn't apply here if I didn't," he said, not wanting to add *I can't get a job anywhere else at the moment, short of a diner.* "I'm looking for a change."

Her eyebrow quirked up expressively. "This isn't a change. This is a step down for someone of your…stature." Her tone was sarcastic. "And the job is a sous-chef, not a head chef. We've already got one of those here." She paused. "Me."

He shrugged. Head chef or no, she could use a good second-in-command chef-chef, from the looks of the chaotic kitchen. "I don't mind." It was just temporary, anyway.

"Well, I do," she said, and her tone turned sharp. "I don't need a chef who's got a lot of credentials and just yells orders. I need a working line chef, somebody who can get it done. Not somebody who just looks good in a suit."

"Leon Grunning sent me," he drawled, keeping his anger at bay. "If I could work for him, I suppose I could manage to make myself useful."

Her expression softened immediately. "Leon sent you?"

"He'll give you a letter of recommendation if you need one."

She shook her head. "I'll just give him a call. I was going to call him at the end of this week, anyway," she said, surprising Nick. Leon had been a tough son of a bitch as a teacher, and few students stayed in contact with him. He wondered when Mari had graduated—and how she herself had done in the CSA's rigorous program.

"Okay." She got up off the desk.

"Okay, I have the job?"

"Okay, you get a trial run." She adjusted her apron. "Leon's word means a lot to me…but the restaurant means a lot more. I see how you work with my crew first, then you're in."

Five years with a top-ranked restaurant, and here he

was, trying out like some novice? *Oh, man, if I didn't need this job…*

But he did need this job.

"When do I start?"

She looked him up and down. "Well, tonight's as good a night as any."

He stared down at his clothes, aghast. This was a Prada suit, for God's sake! "Tonight? But I'm not dressed…"

She grinned, and he realized she was taking acute pleasure in his discomfort, so he shut his mouth. She was trying to prove a point. Well, he would pay for dry-cleaning. Hell, he'd sacrifice the suit if he had to. When his plans were finished, he'd be able to buy five more if he wanted. "Tonight's fine," he said curtly.

"Great." She walked over to a cupboard, pulled out an apron and a chef's toque, a smaller hat than he was used to. "You'll be working the line…setting up the 'meez', expediting orders, whatever else I need you to do," she said.

The "meez" or mise-en-place was the setup of basic ingredients. So she was going to have him chopping onions and the like, and calling out orders.

He'd show her, he thought.

He pulled off his coat and placed it on the desk. Then he removed his suit jacket and rolled up his sleeves, pulling on the apron. "Where do you want me?" he said.

She smiled, a wicked, sensual smile that he was sure was unconscious, even if it sent a blast of heat through his system.

"I haven't determined if I want you yet or not," she said slowly, the smile mocking him. "But you'll be the first to know."

He was tired, too tired to play games. He stepped up to her until they were only inches apart, gratified by the way her eyes widened like saucers.

"Trust me," he said, in a low voice. "You'll want me."

They stood like that for a moment, face to face, challenging. And could have cooked something just from the sudden, inexplicable heat between them.

She was the one who broke eye contact first. Her smile faltered slightly, then came back in full force.

"Well, then...*stud*," she said. "Get on with it. Let's see if you're everything you think you are."

MARI COULD STILL FEEL the heat from Nick's gaze, an hour later, sequestered in the back room with her best friend and the restaurant's business manager, Lindsay.

"He certainly is good looking," Lindsay said, with her usual understated tone. "But can he cook?"

Mari nodded. "He's not just a pretty face, from what I've seen. He's efficient, he's thorough, and he seems to know what he's doing."

Lindsay smiled demurely. Her shoulder-length blond bob was streaked with highlights, but her crystal-sharp green eyes were shrewd. "And you want him."

Boy, do I ever, Mari thought, then shook it off. That wasn't what Lindsay was asking—that wasn't something Lindsay would ask. "Yeah. Ever since Rinaldo quit to move to New York, we've been running short-handed, and I've been making up the difference. I'd like to start sleeping again." She'd like to start sleeping *with* someone again. Although at this point in her restaurant's nascent stages, only six months in business, a social life still seemed out of the question. She looked at the sleek black laptop Lindsay had propped up on the scarred desk surface. "The question is—can I afford him?"

Lindsay's brow furrowed with concentration. "It doesn't look good, I have to tell you that," she said. "We haven't picked up enough business, Mari. You're maintaining a decent profit margin, but we're not putting out enough meals."

If anybody would be able to tell the future of a restaurant's business, it would be Lindsay…not only was she an MBA and a crack accountant, her parents had owned a restaurant since Lindsay was a kid, and Lindsay's head for numbers had revealed itself at an early age. Mari took a glance at the spreadsheet, and nodded grimly. "So I can't hire him?" That caused a pang—and not just from the standpoint of finally getting some rest.

She hated to admit it, but he was *very* good looking. And, just as sexy, he was a hell of a cook. For someone as interested in the culinary arts as Mari, the way a man handled himself in the kitchen was an indication of how he handled himself elsewhere.

She got the feeling Nick would be an expert in the kitchen…and other places.

She shook the thought off, waiting for Lindsay's response.

Lindsay took a deep breath, and Mari could almost see the calculations working in her eyes. "If you hired him at base pay, you could probably manage," Lindsay said slowly.

"Base pay?" Mari shook her head. "Have you seen the guy's resumé? Four Seasons, Blackstone's. He was managing Le Chapeau Noir, for pity's sake."

Lindsay's eyes narrowed. "Yeah. What happened there, anyway? I get the feeling he got fired."

Mari thought about it. "I don't know."

"You don't know?" Lindsay's eyes widened. "Don't you think that's something you ought to investigate before you think about hiring someone? He could be an embezzler or something...."

"Or he could have been set up by his partner," Mari said in a flat tone of voice.

Lindsay stopped, her sharp gaze softening. "You know I didn't mean that," she said, her voice gentle. "I know how hard it was for you to get a job...after the whole Le Pome nightmare."

Mari winced just to hear the name of the restaurant she used to run...one that had gone out of business in a spectacular burst of failure, thanks to the owner's mismanagement and her own naive need to please. "An old teacher of mine recommended him," she said instead. "He needs a chance. And he's good... I'm not just saying that."

Lindsay bit her lip, then nodded. "Well, if he accepts base pay, then I'll add him to payroll."

"Don't worry," Mari said, feeling a knot of tension she didn't realize she was holding loosen in her chest. "I'll persuade him."

"If anyone could, it'd be you." Lindsay smiled, but Mari could still see concern haunting the corners of it.

"Lindsay," Mari said, in a low voice. "How bad is it, really?"

The smile slipped away. "If things don't change," she said, in an emotionless tone, "I give us four months. And that's on the outside."

Mari blanched. "I knew things weren't going well…"

"The lease is going to need to be renewed then, and there's a good chance rent will go up. And we were hoping more business would come in, now that spring's here and summer's coming," Lindsay said. "But we need to do something. I don't know. Promotion, maybe." She looked at Mari, her tone hesitant. "I know a restaurant critic with the *Chronicle*…"

"No critics." Mari's reaction was swift and reflexive.

Lindsay took a deep breath. This was one point Mari could never really get across to her. "Mari, it's the cheapest form of promotion…."

"Yeah. And you can't guarantee the results." Mari closed her eyes, remembering the critics' response to Le Pome: *The culinary equivalent of "Bonfire of the Vanities", Le Pome is an overpriced, overhyped, pretentious nightmare of a restaurant.* She winced. "We get a critic who decides to make his name by tearing us to shreds with some humorously deadly review, and we're nailing the coffin shut, Lindsay.''

Lindsay put her hands up. "Okay. I'm sorry.''

Mari closed her eyes. Lindsay meant well. But her restaurant was her life—and talking to critics had killed her last dream, and she wasn't eager to rush out and go through that again. "Let me think about it, at least.''

Lindsay took the concession, and quickly rushed on. "I don't know. You might want to work on a new menu, too. Tweak it a little.''

Mari nodded. She'd thought about doing that, anyway. "Will do.''

"Maybe get that new chef to help you?''

Mari thought about it. Nick, with his expensive suit and his slow smile...and those very hot gazes of his. He knew he was good. Back when she was in school, they called guys like Nick "celebrities.'' He wouldn't be happy with being a sous-chef for long, and she got the feeling if she gave him a chance to work on the menu, he'd parlay it into a chance to take over her kitchen.

She glanced at the door that led to the kitchen, smiling at the din of pots, pans and yelled conversations. *Like hell.* The kitchen, the restaurant, was hers...and hers alone.

"Let me just see if I can get the guy to accept base pay,'' Mari said. "We'll worry about the rest later.''

Mari washed her hands, taking the time to collect herself. She had the feeling that Nick could be a blessing or a curse for Guilty Pleasures—or both. Even if she could afford to hire Nick, she wasn't sure she could afford the distraction. When she got a glimpse of him, her senses seemed to go into erotic overdrive. And as much fun as it might sound, making a sensual feast of her sous-chef was probably the *last* thing she needed.

The only guilty pleasures she indulged in at the moment were on her menu.

It was eleven, and the crew was cleaning up to close for the night. She had to admit, the kitchen looked cleaner and more organized than it had in a while, even if her tight-knit crew looked more surly than usual. Nick was calling out orders, but not in a supercilious way, and the whole time, he was a blur of motion, straightening something here, putting something away there.

She must've been staring for some time, because she didn't even hear Mo come up behind her. "Isn't he delicious?" Mo whispered.

Apt description. "Yes, but is he competent?" she whispered back, sounding blasé.

"I'll bet he is," Mo purred.

Getting his connotation, she smirked. "I meant in the kitchen, Mo."

Mo stood next to her, winking. "I'm sure he's competent *wherever.*"

"At *cooking,* you imbecile," Mari said, laughing.

Mo snorted. "All work and no play…"

"Keeps us solvent." She shooed Mo away, and walked up to Nick. "So. Looks like you're as good as you say you are,'' she drawled, grinning at the sauce stains and splotches on his previously immaculate shirt.

His tawny eyes looked like brandy and banked fires. ''I'm better,'' he said, in a low, rough-husky voice. ''But this was only one night.''

She ignored the shiver his statement sent up her spine.

''So did I pass the test?'' he asked.

She noticed that the crew had quieted and was listening to their exchange with interest. She remembered Lindsay's question in the back room…about whether he'd been fired or was an embezzler.

She needed to interview him. In private.

''Grab your coat.'' She gestured to the back room, then looked at Tiny, her grill man, and Mo. ''I want the logs and checklists ready when I get back to lock up, okay? I'm just going to talk to Nick over at my office.''

They nodded, although Mo was grinning like a fiend.

He walked out, putting his coat on, and she grabbed hers as well. ''Where is your office?''

She shot him a quick smirk. ''Across the street,'' she said, and waved a quick goodbye to the crew, who were grinning too.

She was taking him to her home office…to her loft, across the street.

I am going to be alone with a gorgeous man who makes my hormones do back flips. At eleven o'clock at night. In the middle of a rainstorm.

She felt her pulse rate raise a little. *In the general vicinity of my bed.*

No, no, no. She stepped out into the rain, letting the cooling waves of it turn her temperature down a little. She was just going to hire him…and convince him to take the salary she offered. She got the feeling it was going to take every ounce of charm and persuasion she possessed.

This was for the restaurant, she told herself sternly as she opened the door to her building. Sex would only get in the way.

NICK FOLLOWED MARI to the industrial-looking brick building across the street. It looked like it held lofts…or those work spaces.

Is she taking me to where she lives, then? Is that what all the grinning in the kitchen had been about?

Not that he would have minded accompanying this particular woman home. It had been months since he'd broken up with Janelle, it hadn't lasted long, and he really hadn't had the time or the inclination to be with a woman since. And Mari was woman with a capital W. He could tell from the easy stride of her gait that she moved with determination and a very seductive grace.

Still, she could move like an exotic dancer and look like a sexual goddess, he thought as he walked up the two flights of stairs that led to her place. The fact was, she'd made him "try out" to work at her dubious restaurant. Now that he'd proven how capable he was, it was her turn.

As the movie said, she had to show him the money. And he might be available, but if he ever wanted to get his place back in the restaurant world, he wasn't going to come cheap.

She unlocked the door, and turned on a light. He followed her inside.

He didn't know what he was expecting, but the roomy loft wasn't it. It was painted in rich autumn hues, although the ceiling still showed exposed steel beams. The main "room" was painted in a warm pumpkin tone, rich and exotic. There were colorful forest green and burgundy tapestry pillows on an over-stuffed couch. He walked to the center of the living room while she went to a large oak desk strewn with paper. There was a small but well-appointed kitchen, he noticed, and suspended over it was a "floor," about seven feet up, with a ladder leading up to it. While someone probably had used it for storage be-fore, from his vantage point, he could make out some gauzy type material, curtains and pillows.

That's where she sleeps.

He felt the slight stirrings of an erection, *not* what he needed to go into a negotiation with. He turned, and looked out the huge floor-to-ceiling windows in-stead. The neighborhood wasn't much to look at, but it had a view of the sign's wink and grin.

When he felt he had his body under control, he focused on the live model instead…and almost promptly wished he hadn't.

She reached up and pulled her hair from its restrain-ing rubber band, letting it tumble across her shoulders in unruly ebony waves. The purple streak seemed to fit the room, he noted, and matched the violet-blue of her eyes.

She was a powerfully beautiful woman.

"So." She leaned back against the desk, her long legs crossing at the ankle. "Why won't anybody else hire you, Nick Avery?"

He took a deep breath. A beautiful, no-punches-pulled kind of woman.

"I told you. I need a change."

Her eyebrow arched up. "I didn't just come in off the bus from the country, Nick."

He sighed. He knew it wasn't going to be that easy—it hadn't been anywhere else. And with a woman this sharp, he shouldn't have tried. "I left Le Chapeau Noir in less than ideal circumstances."

"I'd gathered," she said dryly. She paused. "Embezzlement?"

"No." The word was harsh, but the idea of it punched him in the gut. He thought about sitting, but didn't want to get too comfortable. "There were no legal charges filed."

She narrowed her eyes now, crossing her arms. And he saw the look that he'd been getting in every other interview that he'd been in for the past month.

"What exactly did you do?"

I trusted my best friend. I got screwed.

He clenched his jaw, forced himself to relax. He was at the end of the line. "I supposedly stole from the restaurant—thousands of dollars worth of food, comped meals, equipment. Somebody suggested I had my hand in the till, but wouldn't go that far.''

That somebody being Phillip Marceau—his business partner and best friend.

''I see.'' Her expression changed, but he couldn't read it. He waited for more, for judgments, but none came. She simply studied him silently.

''I didn't do any of it.'' Once the words were out, he winced. He hadn't defended himself against Phillip's whispered allegations, hinted at by people he interviewed with, because he knew the fraternity of high-society, four-star restaurants would take the word of the powerful Marceau restaurant family over the word of a one-time poor kid from Covina.

So why had he wanted her to know he was innocent?

''They didn't press charges?'' she asked instead.

''No. They didn't. He—my old business partner— said they were doing it to protect my reputation…because I'd meant so much to his family.'' He didn't mean for that much bitterness to creep into his voice, but couldn't seem to help it.

''And you tried here.''

''Because of Leon,'' he reminded her. He smiled, thinking of the conversation, and she picked up on it.

''What?''

He shrugged. ''He said this was a good place for me to get a second chance, that's all.'' Leon had been a tough teacher, but he had to admit, the man was a good friend. Right now, Nick had a short supply of those.

The look on her expressive face was something to see. "He said that? That part about the second chance?"

Nick nodded, puzzled.

She started laughing, although her brilliant violet eyes didn't reflect the humor. "That crafty old bastard."

"Sorry?"

"Okay, Nick Avery." She rumpled her hair, took a deep breath. "You're hired."

He smiled, feeling his shoulders release their tension. "You won't regret it."

"See that I don't," she said, then stood up, smiling at him almost flirtatiously. "Of course, I can only offer base scale."

He blinked. He took a step closer to her, keeping a leash on his anger. "I think I'm worth more than that," he said, his voice low and reasonable. "Give me a few weeks, and I'm sure I could convince you that I am."

She took a step to meet him, her smile not wavering. "Oh, I'm sure you're worth more than that."

His body was responding again, but he ignored it and focused on his anger instead. "But you know I can't get a job anywhere else, so…?"

That managed to irk her. "I don't do that," she said, her voice sharp and her eyes snapping with electricity. "I wouldn't do that. But facts are facts: I'm taking a risk here. I want to give you a second chance. But I've got to protect myself—and my restaurant."

He grimaced at that. "Maybe we could negotiate," he said, in his best charm-the-owner voice.

"Well...maybe we could. Hmm." She got a look of innocent thoughtfulness, and his guard immediately went up. "But I'd have to be *sure*. Say, a three-month trial period?"

Another trial period. Just when he thought things couldn't get any more insulting.

She leaned forward slightly, her mouth curving into a very sweet, sexy smile. "Three months in my kitchen. That's not a very long time, is it?" She winked. "I'll even go easy on you."

He found himself mesmerized by her body language, and shook it off. "Ms. Salazar," he said, pitching his own voice low and husky, "are you trying to con me?"

She blinked, then let out a warm laugh. "No. But I'll put it this way. I want you, Nick."

Now his body clenched, tightly.

She shut her eyes, and to his surprise, he saw the dull stain of a blush high on her cheeks. She turned back to the desk. "For the restaurant," she hastily amended. "I think that we could be very good for each other, Nick. I want to help. But I can only hire you at base pay." She looked at him over her shoulder, her posture unconsciously provocative. "Take it or leave it."

Suddenly, he wanted to take more than the job.

He let out a low, quavering breath, and put out his hand. "I'll take it."

She turned, her smile megawatt-bright and beautiful. She took his hand.

He lingered over the handshake, enjoying the warmth of her palm.

She finally tugged away. "We're open Tuesday through Sunday," she said. Was she breathless, or did he just imagine it? "Lunch and dinner only. I'm there by nine, I usually work both shifts. When do you want to start?"

"As soon as possible," he said. *Right now, for instance.*

"All right. Tomorrow?"

"Tomorrow. I'll be there at nine."

She took a deep breath "One last thing. "You'll be my sous-chef, and I'll rely on you as my second-in-command. But it's still my kitchen, and my restaurant. My call. Clear?"

"As crystal," he murmured.

"Oh. One last thing."

He quirked an eyebrow, then his eyes widened as she took a step closer to him, leaning up to whisper in his ear. Her proximity, and the floral yet spicy scent of her, caught him off guard. The front of her thighs brushed against his, causing a jolt to course through his system. Suddenly his heart was pounding, making it difficult for him to stand.

"I'm trusting you because Leon does," she whispered, the soft brush of her breath against his skin making him want to hold her to him. "But this restaurant is my life. You do *anything* to jeopardize my restaurant, and what happened to you at Le Chapeau

Noir is going to seem like a walk in the park. Don't think I'm kidding. You got it?''

He looked down into her eyes…deep violet, intense as flame.

"Some day you'll learn to trust me on your own," he replied softly, then did what he'd wanted to do since he'd walked into her restaurant…he leaned forward, brushing his lips against hers, savoring the petal-softness of her full mouth.

She let out a low sound, something like a moan.

This was a bad idea, he thought…until she pressed forward, matching her mouth to his own.

The kiss was slow, rich as chocolate, hot as fire. They didn't hold each other, didn't grasp at each other…simply brushed mouth against mouth in a slow, exotic play of tastes and textures.

When she pulled away, it was a shock to his system, and he reeled to get balance back.

"I may trust you someday," she said, taking a step back. He noticed she was trembling slightly. "But today's not that day, Nick. I'll see you in the morning. Now, I've got to get back to my restaurant.''

2

—————

IT WAS EIGHT-THIRTY in the morning on Sunday, and Mari was at work extra early. Not that there was extra preparation that needed to be done—Sundays were notoriously slow, and she could get inventory and her orders for the week done in the course of regular business. But she hadn't slept well, and she'd been restless. Now, she was working on developing a new menu, trying to think of a new theme. Trying to get rid of some excess energy by focusing on her beloved restaurant.

Why did you let him kiss you?

She closed her eyes, putting down the pear that she'd been about to slice. That was the reason she was restless—why she hadn't been able to sleep. Yes, he was gorgeous. Yes, he was sexy. She'd known gorgeous and sexy men before—she'd even worked with one or two.

She'd never kissed one within hours of meeting him. And certainly not after she'd *hired* him.

She rubbed her eyes with her hands. Apparently, she hadn't been thinking at all. She'd been trying to intimidate him, she supposed…at least, that was her excuse for getting that close to him. Then he'd kissed her. Worse, she'd *kissed him back.*

Her lips tingled just at the memory of it. And a kiss had never had *that* effect on her before.

She shook herself mentally. In striking her bargain with him, she'd bought herself time—she could have him for base pay for three months. If the restaurant turned around and made a profit, she could offer him more. If it didn't, then a raise wouldn't matter...none of them would have a job. She had to focus all of her energy on ensuring that situation didn't happen.

The last thing she needed was to get sidetracked by her bizarre physical attraction to the very sexy Nick Avery.

''Hi there.''

She looked up. *Speak of the devil.*

Nick stood in the open back doorway. His clothing emulated the rest of the crew's normal attire: long-sleeved T-shirt, a pair of black, loose-fitting slacks, comfortable shoes. The only difference was his shirt didn't sport one of the humorous slogans her crew normally wore.

Well, that and the fact that the muscles of his chest and shoulders seemed to pull the fabric taut, in a very enticing way. His light brown hair was still damp from a shower.

Nick in the shower...

''You're early,'' she said, displeased with the unruliness of her thoughts. ''Shift doesn't start till nine.''

He shrugged. ''Thought I'd come in early, get any

paperwork you might have out of the way. And maybe you could give me the layout of the kitchen.''

''You worked here last night. It's a small kitchen.'' She didn't mean to sound curt, but after tossing and turning all night with restless thoughts about him, the kitchen was *definitely* too small to be alone with him. ''I'll go get your paperwork.''

To her dismay, he followed her into the miniscule back room. He seemed to take up all the remaining space between them. She was having trouble breathing, it seemed. She opened a desk drawer, pulling out the paperwork Lindsay had meticulously filed. ''Just fill it out and leave it here,'' she said, hating the breathless quality of her voice. ''Lindsay will take care of it when she comes in tomorrow. She's the only one who works on Mondays. Says it's quieter.''

Now I'm babbling. She forced herself to shut up, and headed for the door.

He was in her way. ''I wanted to apologize.''

She stared at him. He looked sincere. ''I assume you mean for last night?''

''Yes.'' His voice was like warm fingers, caressing her skin. ''I shouldn't have initiated that...well, you know.''

''Forget it,'' she said. ''I already have.''

His eyebrow quirked up in an aristocratic arch. He didn't believe her. Why should he? She was lying right down to her toes.

''Happen often?'' he asked with deceptive casualness.

She bristled slightly at that. ''No. In fact...'' She

bit her tongue. She didn't need to admit how long it had been since she'd had the time to get physical with a man. "I just think it'll be easier for both of us if we just put the whole incident out of our minds. Okay?"

He nodded, stepping to one side. She walked out into the kitchen, which felt degrees cooler than the back room, where Nick seemed to generate his own heat. Too quickly, he was out in the kitchen, again. Her body knew it even before she saw him walk towards her.

He glanced down at the hasty, impromptu sketches and nearly illegible scrawls on her notepad. "New recipes?" he asked.

She felt her guard snap into place, and shrugged. "Just kicking around a few new ideas," she said. "I'm thinking of changing the menu. We need a new theme."

He frowned. "What exactly would you call the theme now?"

She was irritated at his question—and since irritation was better than arousal in this particular instance, she latched onto the emotion and held tight. "I didn't want to create another bourgeois restaurant, with a bunch of pretentious-sounding items and weird flavors just for the sake of being creative," she said, more vehemently than perhaps she'd intended. But it was a familiar rant. "I wanted to create foods that people liked, but couldn't get on the menu at any of the other trendy restaurants. That's how we came up with the name—Guilty Pleasures." She smiled now, remembering the debate that had taken place between herself,

Lindsay and Mo when they'd chosen the name. "It's a place where you go to get what you crave, but which isn't necessarily en vogue."

He stared at her. "Feel pretty passionately about that, huh?"

She felt a little blush start up, and laughed at herself. "Sorry. You hit a hot button. But everybody who works here knows my stance on this."

"So that's why you cook what you do…pan-fried chicken with sweet Meyer lemonade, mashed Yukon Gold potatoes with gravy, ice cream sundaes." His voice was contemplative. "Favorites, but nothing really trend-setting."

She glared at him for that one, and now it was his turn to look uncomfortable. "That wasn't an insult," he said quickly. "That was just an observation."

"At any rate, I'm going to be working on it," she said, ignoring the sting that his "observation" wrought. "It should be an easy day—we close early, at nine. We don't get a lot of business on Sundays."

She got the feeling he realized they didn't get a whole lot of business on the other days, either. "I could help with the menu," he suggested. "I developed several at Le Chapeau Noir, after all."

She picked up her notepad. "Thanks, but I think I can manage."

"Sometimes it helps to have someone to brainstorm with," he said, his tone mild. "That's all I'm saying."

Maybe she was being unreasonable, but she knew men like Nick—ambitious, go-getters. Especially thwarted ones. If she gave the man an inch, he'd take her whole kitchen. Her whole *restaurant*. At least, that's what he'd act like.

"I'll manage," she reiterated. "But thanks for offering."

She tried to start sketching again, but she couldn't with him staring at her...and she could feel his gaze like a touch. "What?" She finally asked, turning to look at him.

His arms were crossed, making his pectoral muscles flex a bit. "Is it just me you have a problem with, or do you not accept help from anyone?"

She put down the notebook with a slap. "For your first day on the job, don't you think it's unwise to start off by pushing my buttons?"

"I don't mean to," he said, his eyes lazy and low-lidded. "But you hired me to help your restaurant...and now you're turning my help away. I was just wondering if this was another trust issue, or if you're like this with everyone."

She started to let out a sharp retort, bit back on it. Then she let out a low, impatient breath. It really wasn't his fault. Well, the fact that she was on edge was definitely his doing, granted...but this was a little different. "I had a bit of a bad experience, a while back," she said slowly. A brief memory of Le Pome flashed across her mind. "Let's just say it was like menu by committee. And in trying to please everyone, I betrayed myself. So from here on out, I create the menus here."

He nodded, and from the look on his face, it seemed like he really understood. She felt the tension between her shoulders relax a little bit. "Nothing personal," she said, finally.

"Gotcha." He glanced again at the top sketch, and tapped it. "Poached pear in spiced honey sauce, huh?"

She had to stop herself from gaping at him. "You can read that?"

He nodded, not looking at her. "Have you considered going with more Moroccan flavors, rather than just cinnamon and nutmeg?"

Before she could stop him, he picked up a pencil and started drawing what he had in mind, listing off various ingredients: cardamon, cloves, and paprika. "It'll be a little spicy for a dessert," he mused. "Maybe something cool…and creamy, to counterbalance? I'm thinking maybe whipped cream with a hint of sherry, or possibly a cool sorbet. What do you think?"

She looked over his sketch, imagining what he had in mind. "That's not bad," she said, glancing up at him, and then caught her breath at the sexy, confident grin on his face.

"I'm not bad either," he said in a low voice. "Why don't you give me a try?"

Her heart started pounding in her chest. Suddenly, she wanted very badly to give him a try.

"Let me cook for you," he said. "You seem very fond of trial runs. Let me see if I can impress you enough to help out."

She blinked. Of course he wasn't offering anything

else. So why was her body reacting with such disappointment?

She heard the bustling of the crew coming in…the morning shift was here. She took one last peek at the sketch.

"Okay," she said grudgingly. After all, she was going to be creating a whole new menu. Maybe she was being unreasonable. At the very least, she could let him think he was getting a fair trial, before telling him that, as always, she'd be coming up with the menu on her own.

"Great." He leaned toward her, and she hoped nobody had come into the kitchen yet. "How does tonight sound?"

Her mouth went dry. "Tonight? For what?"

"I'll cook for you."

That shouldn't have sounded sexy, but from his mouth, it sounded downright sinful.

"Just give me a chance. You'll be hungry, so I'll whip up something for dinner for you."

"All right," she said, slowly. "But it'll have to be quick…I'm going to have a night crew doing a thorough cleaning of the kitchen."

"Why don't I cook it at your place, then?" Although his voice sounded reasonable, the heat coming from his eyes was intense. "Just cook," he assured her. "And then we won't be…rushed."

She took a deep breath. The crew would be in any second.

"All right," she heard herself say. "After work tonight. Although after a twelve-hour shift, I doubt you're going to feel up to anything really challenging.''

He grinned at her. "You'd be surprised at my stamina," he murmured. "See you tonight."

"Hey, boss," Tiny, her grill man for the morning shift, said in a gravelly voice. "You got last night's logs?"

"I'll go get them," she said, hurrying for the back room. She shot one last quick look at Nick.

His eyes never left her. She turned back to the makeshift office, grabbing the log books.

What the hell have I agreed to?

NICK WALKED THROUGH the inventory and supplies with Tiny, the ill-named grill man. At six foot one and easily two hundred and fifty pounds, Tiny was an enormous black man with a flopping chef's "toque" or hat, and a glinting gold earring. He grinned widely and spoke in a slow, deep bass voice. Still, Nick noted what the man said, absently checking things off on his own makeshift list. If he were at Le Chapeau, he'd be coming up with specials, noting what needed to be tossed, thinking of how to improve cost and maybe kicking around a few new recipe ideas.

Now, he could just think of tonight—cooking for Mari.

What the hell was I thinking?

He looked over, between the moving bodies of chefs, to see Mari in her element, pan-frying chicken on the busy sauté station, her mouth curving into a sensual smile at some joke that the young pastry cook,

Zooey, was telling. He watched as she deftly plated the meal, shutting the reach-in pantry drawer with her hip. She looked over, catching his gaze on her, and he could have sworn her violet eyes darkened for a second before hastily looking away. His body reacted with a characteristic tightening.

The thing was, he *wasn't* thinking. Not with his head, anyway.

Okay, not with that head.

''Nick? You still with me?''

He shifted his attention back to Tiny. ''Sorry. Was thinking up some possible specials,'' he lied.

Tiny frowned. ''Mari comes up with the menus. Including the specials.''

This, at least, was able to shift Nick's focus. ''I'm the sous-chef. I go over the inventory, mark what's low. I was just thinking I could help by suggesting a couple of specials....''

''That's not what Mari hired you for,'' Tiny said, in a tone that would have been intimidating even if the guy weren't built like a line backer.

I'm going to have a problem here.

He'd been so fixated on Mari, he hadn't really paid attention to the rest of the crew. Now, he realized that most of them were casting suspicious glances his way. He felt sure that Mari hadn't mentioned anything to them about the allegations from Le Chapeau Noir...he'd only told her last night, and he'd arrived before anyone this morning.

Which meant that they didn't trust him for other reasons.

"So. How long have you known Mari?" he asked Tiny, trying to start off friendly, at least.

"We worked together a couple of years ago. She was just a dishwasher when I met her. We hit it right off. She said I was the best grill man she'd ever seen." He grinned with pride at this, revealing a gold-capped tooth. "So when she opened up the restaurant and asked me to come, I came. I knew that she had her act together, you know? And she runs a tight ship. She doesn't take crap from anybody."

He gave Nick a meaningful look. *So don't try giving her any,* the expression seemed to say.

Nick nodded. "And everybody else here…?"

"She's made a lot of friends," Tiny said, shrugging. "Most of us have worked together over the years, at different times."

"Small world," Nick said, with only a hint of irony.

Tiny shrugged again. "So. We've got a lot of chicken to move…not everybody's buying the pan-fry." Nick noticed Tiny was trying not to sound concerned by this.

"Hmm. Maybe we could try something a little different…maybe a little more exotic," he mused. "Chicken with Molé Poblano, maybe."

"It's up to Mari," Tiny repeated. "Let's go over the walk-in."

Nick listened dutifully as Tiny went over the stores in the walk-in pantry, but inwardly he seethed. He wasn't going to be much more than a grocery clerk and assistant line-chef at this rate, if the crew didn't recognize his authority. Obviously Mari's "this is my kitchen" philosophy was bred deep.

The restaurant was obviously in trouble. He could tell that from how many supplies weren't moving. He could help her, dammit, if only she'd let him.

And you could help yourself. A few of his dishes on the menu, and the responsibility for turning around a failing restaurant, would go a long way toward rebuilding his tarnished reputation.

"Thanks, Tiny," he said, when Tiny was finished with his tour.

"Now you'll want to meet the crew," Tiny said. So Nick met all of them: Zooey, the dimunitive blond pastry chef; Paulo, the sauté cook; Juan, the prep cook and self-proclaimed soup guy; Miguel, the runner and garde-manger, dishing up salads and cold dishes, getting whatever the chefs needed. All of them met Nick's greeting with a guarded sort of friendliness.

Mari was the last. "Of course, you know me," she said, with a wink and a smile that revealed the dimple in her right cheek.

Not as well as I'm going to.

"Boss," Tiny said, "we got a lot of chicken left over. What do you want me to do with it?"

Nick cleared his throat. "I was thinking we could make some Molé Poblano. It could be a nice addition to the menu."

She looked at him…and the rest of the crew looked at her. This would be an important step. If she accepted his decisions, the crew would follow her lead.

Without breaking eye contact with him, she said,

"Juan? Think you can make some matzo and chicken soup?"

Nick gritted his teeth as Juan cheerfully replied, "Anything you say, boss."

Nick didn't glare at her, but she must have sensed his ire. She addressed the crew at large. "Still, the Molé Poblano's not a bad idea. I'm going to be working on a new menu soon. Paulo, think you might be up for that if I added it?"

Paulo looked at Juan, who was grinning. "I know a great place for fresh chiles, all sorts of varieties. Fresh."

"Fantastic." She walked over to the window, looking out. "In the meantime, work on the soup. And Zooey, the dessert last night went over really well…why don't you make more of those seven-layer cookies?"

Zooey, he noticed, blushed with pride.

"Okay. I'll let you know what I come up with."

With that, the crew went back to business, tossing back conversation over the burners and the bustling. Tiny went back to manning his grill and getting the fryer prepped for the lunch crowd. Unnoticed by the now-busy crew, she sidled up to Nick.

"My kitchen," she whispered, so only he could hear her.

Nick nodded.

For the rest of the day, he worked side-by-side with the crew. If he had been younger, or in another kitchen, what had just happened would have him feeling resentful…and angry. There was a shade of that, he realized. But seeing the way Mari interacted with her crew made him think twice. She bantered back and forth with them, not lording over like some head chefs he'd worked with. She helped out when somebody got "in the weeds," on the few occasions when a flurry of orders came in and a chef got swamped. She wasn't afraid of getting her hands dirty. He admired her for that.

On the other hand, his body seemed constantly aware of her, and that took an edge off his anger, as well. It was hard to stay ticked off at a woman who seemed to unconsciously brush past, a quick smooth rub of hip against leg or chest against back as they maneuvered in the cramped quarters.

It's hard to stay mad when you're ragingly turned on, his mind summed up.

His thoughts turned back to tonight…to the challenge he'd thrown down. He was going to prove a few things to her. Namely, that he needed the authority of second-in-command. That he needed her backing him. That he had the talent to deserve her support.

"Ready on eight. Coming through," Mari sang out, and she moved past him, her soft backside brushing against the front of his crotch as she moved two full plates out of the way.

He gritted his teeth against the sensation that seemed to explode through his body. When she'd put the plates out onto the pickup window, he almost thought he saw her grinning.

He'd show her one other thing, he thought as he turned to the fridge, hoping to cool off his body's blatant reaction. He'd show her that she wasn't the only one who could drive somebody crazy with desire.

He smiled. That was one challenge he was ready for.

MARI HAD NEVER FELT this amped up when closing down the restaurant. She was showing Nick their closing routine: the cleaning of the grills, locking the pantries and freezers, making sure all the burners and lights were turned off and the dishes washed through, going over the best-selling and worst-selling items, locking the deposit in the safe. The restaurant would be closed the next day, and she'd go over the orders and invoices with Lindsay then.

She waved to the last shift crew and left the kitchen to the able hands of Jake, her one-man night cleanup crew. Then, with her skin practically feverish, she turned to Nick.

"All right," she said, making her voice sound as calm, yet cocky as she possibly could. "You ready to show me something?"

She liked the way his eyes lit at the statement. "I hope you're hungry," he said, showing a bag of ingredients that he'd selected from her stores. "I've thought up a couple of things just for you."

"I'm looking forward to it," she drawled, and led the way to her apartment, amazed at the way her stomach danced nervously.

She shouldn't have teased him so much today, she knew that. And to her credit, she hadn't actually *meant* to. She hadn't even said half the double-entendre statements that had flown to mind as he'd gone over the ingredient list so solemnly with Tiny.

There was just something about him, when he went into "I'm-a-top-ranked-chef" mode, that made her want to poke at him. Push him off balance. She knew that the food community was already strangely obsessive about food—hell, she was just as bad, if it came down to it. But he was so deathly *serious,* when it ought to at least be fun. Even knowing that the restaurant could potentially be going down the tubes didn't stop her from being grateful every day that she got to do what she loved.

Then there was his little power-play, she thought, frowning as she unlocked her front door. He was trying to get her tacit approval to change the menu with that whole "why don't we try chicken with Molé Poblano" thing, after she'd told him she created all the menus. She hadn't wanted to have that public a face-off his first day, but he'd pressed the issue. Now, she felt sure he'd try to charm her…seduce her with food, as it were.

She grinned at that, dropping her keys in a pebble-filled bowl by the front door. She'd like to see him try. Sure, he made her senses sing and her common sense jump right out the window…but at the cost of her restaurant?

Fat chance. He could do a strip tease wearing whipped cream, and he'd still get nowhere.

Momentarily, the idea of him naked and wearing some artfully placed whipped cream invaded her mind. She let out a slightly hysterical giggle.

"What's so funny?"

"Sorry," she mumbled, clenching her jaw before another laugh could escape. When she got it under control, she shrugged. "Just remembering a joke Zooey told me."

Okay, so it would be more of a challenge than she was used to, she admitted, watching as he spread out the ingredients on the countertop. Still, she'd be strong. She'd enjoy the spectacle of a gorgeous guy cooking for her in her kitchen. She'd praise his obvious skill.

Then she'd tell him no, in no uncertain terms would he be working on the menu. And send him home.

Without sleeping with him, she reminded herself as he bent down to look in her oven. No matter how nice his ass was.

"This hopefully won't take too long," she said, flopping down in one of her kitchen chairs. "I'm starving."

He turned to treat her to a slow, thoughtful stare. "The best things are worth waiting for," he said, his voice smug. "But don't worry. I won't keep you hungry long."

She watched as he rolled his sleeves up, revealing well-muscled forearms as well as the bulge of his biceps. "Promise?"

His smile was wickedly sensual. "I promise."

Down, girl! She forced herself to focus on what he was cooking. He had the makings of a salad, she noticed, and some gorgonzola. He had a small bag of jasmine rice. He had also grabbed some of the chicken.

Just as well, she thought, her desire and distraction ebbing for a moment. The chicken wasn't selling well. One more thing to worry about.

"So. What am I in for tonight?" she said, hoping to lighten her mood.

His expression was smug. "It's a surprise."

"Hmm." She made a show of looking skeptically at his selection. "I'm still waiting to be impressed."

"Give me time," he murmured.

She watched, and she hated to say it…she *was* impressed. He was deft with a knife, cutting the chicken with almost artistic motions, like it was some sort of martial art. He was showing off, she knew, but he was still damned quick about it, browning the chicken in butter, juicing Meyer lemons, adding white wine and the juice and some capers. The sauce smelled heavenly, and her stomach rumbled in response.

"You're killing me," she said, walking to stand next to him and inhale deeply. "Tell me you're going to be ready soon."

"You keep this up," he said, his eyes glowing, "and I'm going to blindfold you."

She started to make a quick comeback, but he was quicker. "Excuse me," he said, reaching around her to get a bag of pecans. His arm brushed gently against her breasts, and she almost moaned at the quick tightening of her nipples in response. She shot an accusing look at him.

"Sorry," he said, and she could have sworn he

meant it. "You've got a small kitchen. Maybe you should sit at the table?"

His voice was innocent. Still, his eyes smoldered—she wasn't just imagining that.

Considering the unexpected heat currently jetting through her system, she agreed with him. She sat down, giving herself time to cool off...and wonder if maybe this wasn't as bright an idea as she had originally thought.

In a surprisingly short period of time, he said "dinner's on" and presented her with two courses...a pear-and-gorgonzola salad with pecans he'd candied on the stovetop, and lemony chicken piccata.

"This is it?" She felt relief burst through her. Saying no to him would be easier than she'd thought. "A salad and Chicken Piccata? Third graders could make this."

The smug expression didn't waver. "Just taste it first," he said, sitting down with his own plates.

She looked at him dubiously, then took a bite of the salad. The mix of the sharp cheese and the mild pear contrasted with the bitterness of endive, the sourness of the balsamic vinaigrette, and the surprising sweetness of the pecans. She let out a low moan as the taste processed through her mouth, closing her eyes to savor the complexity.

When she opened them, she saw that his eyes were low-lidded and fixed on hers.

"Still simple?" he said mildly.

"Shut up," she said. "I'm having a religious experience."

He grinned and did as told.

They were simple foods—deceptively simple. But the chicken was tender as a dream, and the Meyer lemons made the concoction sweeter than the recipe normally called for. He'd cut the sweetness with olives, unusual for the dish but still a good choice.

He was showing her: *If I can do this with something this basic, imagine what I could do if you let me loose.*

She could just imagine, she thought, studying his smile.

When she finished, she sighed, feeling the warm, sated feeling of someone who had eaten truly inspired good food. "What, no dessert?"

His responding grin made him look boyish. "Are you kidding? Dessert's the best part of the meal."

She batted her eyes at him. "A man after my own heart."

He got up, and she noticed a bag she hadn't seen before. He pulled out a plastic container and a spoon.

"I whipped this up this afternoon, when you were going over receipts with Lindsay. It's a fairly simple recipe, too," he said, "And usually I'd have some whipped cream and raspberries with it. But I think you'll get the idea."

"I don't know," she said, teasing as she dipped the spoon in and stirred the chocolaty-looking concoction. It had swirls to it, light brown curling in dark. "You're getting points off on presentation."

He sat down next to her, scooting his chair so he was closer to her. "Just try some," he said.

She was about to make a comment about his very

preemptory tone when he closed his hand around hers, leading the spoon to her mouth.

It was velvety smooth, a rich blend of dark chocolate and milk chocolate in a substance too light to be called pudding, too creamy to be called mousse. "Oh my," she whispered, closing her eyes and concentrating. This was one of the best desserts she'd had in a long time—since the days of Le Pome. Hell, not even then. She'd grown too accustomed to the heavy Americana childhood desserts they made. This was urbane, she thought.

This was *sexy*.

She realized that his hand was still closed around hers...she could feel the heat of him like an electric charge. She opened her eyes to find him staring at her.

"Aren't you going to have some?" she asked, her voice unsteady.

He nodded, but didn't release her hand. Instead, he took her hand and the spoon it enclosed, and dipped it back into the chocolate. He raised the spoon to his lips, neatly eating some. He smiled with approval, a sensual, inviting smile.

"Is there anything better than chocolate?" he asked.

She could see the answer in his eyes. *There was one thing that was better than chocolate.*

She had a disconcerting feeling that he would be.

And the both of them together...

He leaned forward, just a breath closer. It was déjà vu, just like his "interview," when he'd kissed her.

Her body didn't even wait for him this time. She moved forward and connected.

Mmmm. As she'd suspected, the combined taste of his lips and the haunting hint of chocolate made her growl low in her throat. His tongue traced the inside of her lips, and she moved hers forward, tangling with his, tasting him, taunting him. The pressure of his lips increased, and she didn't back down.

He reached across the table, grasping her arms in a gentle but inescapable grip. He tugged, and she found herself off her own chair, and straddling him on his chair. She looked down to find his toffee-brown eyes surveying her solemnly.

"Would you believe me if I told you this wasn't my intent?" he rasped, tugging her lower onto what felt like a sizeable erection.

"Would you believe me if I told you I swore I wouldn't do this?" she said, before moving forward, her breasts crushing against his chest. She moved her hips as she swallowed his groan, devouring his mouth with her own. Her heart rate had escalated to the point of frenzy…her hands roamed his shoulders, his chest, while she grew damp at the feeling of his hardness between her thighs. The sound of his low moans and the way he clutched at her hips only increased the fever-pitch.

With what little sanity she had left, she tore away, breathing hard. "This is crazy," she muttered, starting to get up, only to have him stand with her and scoop her up, carrying her over to the couch. She was laughing until he stroked the undersides of her breasts, moving to circle her now oversensitized nipples.

"I don't understand it either," Nick responded, smiling in response as she arched forward so he could cup her more fully. "On the other hand, I'm not complaining."

Her chuckles were breathless. "This doesn't impact what you get to put on the menu, you realize." She didn't wait for him to reply, just tugged him down on top of her, pressing her into the soft cushions of her couch. Her jeans-clad legs wrapped around his waist, relishing the weight that was pressing against her.

She could feel his laughter, hot breath against her skin. "I'd think less of you if it could," he answered. Then he stopped speaking. He was moving his hips against hers, mimicking sex, as he pressed suckling kisses against her neck. When he nibbled on her earlobe, she gasped as sensations trembled through her.

Her leg climbed higher on his hip, desperate for contact with him where she most needed it. "Nick," she breathed. "I want you."

"I've wanted you since I saw you," he said in between hard kisses. "You have no idea."

"I think I've got a pretty good idea." She pushed him away for a second, to tug her shirt over her head.

He stared at her breasts, cupped in the lacy bra that she'd pulled out this morning. She hadn't planned this, but since she'd kissed him, she had to admit that she'd felt sexier…and the lingerie she pulled out of her drawer on a whim suddenly made sense. Still, he didn't do anything, just looked.

She finally started to squirm under his rapt attention. "I haven't shocked you, have I?" she asked, embarrassment causing the heat of a blush to start from her toes and work its way up. "I don't usually do this, I swear. I just…"

"You're beautiful," he said. "I…you're sure, right?"

She looked into his eyes, and for the first time since she'd met him, she saw the uncertainty in his usually confident eyes.

Instead of answering him, she reached up, cupping his face. Then tugged him down for a slow, warm, lingering kiss.

He must have believed her, she thought dreamily as he moved down from her mouth to the hollow of her throat, then lower. She almost cried when he sucked on her, dampening the silky cloth of her bra and teasing her breasts with feather-light strokes of his fingers. She was trembling, actually *shivering*. Her panties had to be soaked.

She wanted to be nakcd, twined around this man, she realized. Now.

"Mari," he whispered against her skin, leaning up to taste her mouth again. And reached for the fly of her jeans.

She shivered her way out of her jeans, smiling as his eyes widened at the high French-cut bikini panties that matched the bra.

"Your turn," she murmured, tugging off his shirt. Then she stopped. She had to.

The guy was *magnificent.* She gaped at the smooth, muscular perfection of his torso.

His eyes were like bonfires as he reached for her, tracing the lacy edges of her panties. "I've thought about what you were hiding under those clothes of yours," he said. "But I see my imagination didn't do you justice."

"Likewise," she said, fingering his corded muscles with the pads of her fingers. "All this, and you can cook, too."

His smirk was dark, mysterious. "And that's not all."

With that, she felt one of his strong fingers push the panties out of the way, stroking her clitoris with a firm, sure stroke. She gasped.

"Tell me what you like," he murmured, continuing to lick at her breasts as his finger continued its maddening exploration of her sex. A second finger pressed in deeper, past her clit, enveloped by her damp heat.

"Oh, yes," she breathed, her hips arching. *"Please…"*

His tongue worked against her nipple as his hands pressed between her legs. She was trembling all over, the feelings of the roughness of his fingers against her dampness and the velvet heat of his mouth against her breasts combining in a state of sensual overload.

She felt the tremors start before she recognized what they were…and by the time she did realize what was happening, the orgasm had ripped through her mercilessly. She cried out, a throaty moan. "Oh…oh…*Nick!*"

He didn't let up, the relentless motion of both tongue and hand producing an echo of the tremors as he brushed against her G-spot and caused her to almost weep with pleasure.

She collapsed against the couch, limp and sweating. He moved his hand to push himself up on the couch, and she felt bereft at the loss of his fingers pressing inside her.

"When I get the feeling back in my extremities," she said, panting, "I am going to thank you properly."

His grin was smug. "Your response was thanks enough."

"Oh, I'm sure…" she said, then reached for the fly of *his* jeans. "Then I suppose you don't want…'

Rrrrrring.

She glanced over. It was ten o'clock. Who would be calling?

She looked to see Nick staring at the phone, also. She turned his head. "I don't care," she said, lowering the zipper of his pants and smiling as he groaned. She reached in, feeling the length of his erection against the cotton weave of his briefs. It was hard as steel and hot. "Just take me."

But before he could tug the offending material off, the machine clicked on. "Mari? It's Lindsay."

"Ignore it," Mari said, kissing the flat planes of his stomach and edging toward his waistband. She had condoms up in her bed-loft. She would take him upstairs, and they'd finish what they had started.…

"I think I might have figured out something that

might save the restaurant,'' Lindsay's voice said relentlessly.

Despite herself, Mari's attention shifted abruptly to the machine. Unfortunately, so did Nick's.

"Well, maybe not *save*, but definitely help. I was thinking we should enter in a competition. Several of the ones that I've researched offer sizeable cash prizes, and at the very least, they offer very good promotion. They also have a lot of 'guardian angels' at these things—you know, investors. Anyway, we can talk about it tomorrow, but I wanted to call you in case you were home. I didn't want to forget.'' There was a pause. "Of course, we'd only have a few months to pull it off, especially if things don't shape up soon. Still, it's worth thinking about. Call me when you get in…I'll be up.''

There was a click, and the message machine went back to silence.

Mari took a deep breath, staring at Nick, who was now looking at her with an expression she didn't like. "Where were we?'' she said, her hands still in his jeans.

But the mood had shifted. Anyone could tell that.

"Just how much trouble is Guilty Pleasures in, Mari?''

Mari felt the tone of the question like a cold San Francisco fog bank. "It's nothing you need to worry about.''

He leaned back, out of reach of her fingers. "Is it something *you* need to worry about?''

She huffed. "Do we have to talk about this now?''

She nudged herself off the couch, stumbling slightly onto the floor, then turned and glared at him. "I thought we were going to…well, you know."

"That's why you're creating the new menu," Nick said, his tone serious. Obviously the *you know* moment had flown right out the window. "Because you're not moving enough meals or making enough money. Because Guilty Pleasures is going under."

That did it. She grabbed her shirt, tugged it back over her head. "I guess this is the part where I say it's been a lovely evening, and I'll see you at work on Tuesday."

"Mari," he said, standing next to her. Shirtless, with his pants unzipped slightly, he was still enough to make her gasp. "I can help you. I created all the menu plans at Le Chapeau. I was practically the manager. I can help you turn Guilty Pleasures around."

Mari saw the sincerity in his eyes…and yet she saw a hint of something else.

Opportunity, maybe?

"All this, and orgasms, too," she said, her voice sounding bitter to her own ears. "Wow. A woman would have to be a fool to turn that down, huh?"

She paused, then handed him his shirt from the back of the couch.

"Too bad. I've been called a fool so many times, I've got the T-shirt."

He stared at the shirt, then at her. "That's it? You're going to turn me down because you think you don't need my help?"

"No, I'm turning you down because, sous-chef or

not, this is none of your business.'' She tugged on her jeans haphazardly. "I've already done one stupid thing tonight. I'm not going two-for-two. You have a good evening, Nick.''

He pulled his shirt on. "This isn't finished,'' he warned, as she walked past him and opened the door.

She smiled sweetly. "It is for me.'' With that, she closed the door on his glare.

She leaned in, listening to his footsteps as he tromped down the stairs and out into the street.

Who was she kidding? He was right—it wasn't over. In fact, she had the sinking feeling that she'd just started something she wasn't ready for.

3

TUESDAY MORNING, Mari didn't get in to Guilty Pleasures until the last possible moment. She hung back until she saw some of the crew waiting out on the street before crossing and unlocking the door.

She wanted to convince herself that she just needed a little more time to sleep in, but that was a blatant lie—she hadn't slept well since she'd met Nick, and after their interplay Sunday night, she had barely slept at all. She did spend a lot of time in bed…or dreaming, out of bed.

The fact was, she didn't want to be alone with him. Not because she was afraid of him. Rather, she was afraid of what she was going to do when she saw him again.

She *had* been stupid. Unbelievably so. She could remember the quivery aftershocks of really good sex coursing through her like a drug. He'd made her come and he'd promised to help her restaurant.

If she hadn't been burned before, it would have been a promise too good to be true.

Oh sure, he'd help me, she thought. Maybe he was worried about her, and the fortunes of the restaurant. And maybe he meant it, as a charitable gesture.

But she knew that what he was doing wasn't out of the goodness of his heart. He wanted to get ahead, and she might be the one to help him.

There was heat between them, no doubt about it. But however strange and powerful it was, it wasn't "caring"…it was *sex,* pure and simple.

"What's the special?" Xavier said, chalk in hand.

She closed her eyes. "Chicken Piccata," she said, then quickly thought again. "No. Matzo ball soup. Right."

"We've got the makings for either." Xavier shrugged. "Whatever you want, boss."

Whatever I want. She thought of Nick. She couldn't have what she wanted. She shouldn't have even *sampled* what she wanted!

She shifted her feet, while rubbing at her temples. "Let me look at the walk-in, and see what we've got," she said instead.

Of course, she already knew what she had—she'd gone over inventory with Lindsay on Monday, making her orders for the week. But she'd just seen Nick come in, and that was one thing she was not quite ready to deal with.

Hidden away in the coolness of the walk-in pantry, she looked over their stores: cans of artichoke hearts, jars of mayonnaise…the usual supplies. *Maybe chicken salad,* she thought desperately. *Or will that tank like the rest?*

Hell. Maybe she should bite the bullet, and go with that Molé Poblano. It couldn't do worse than anything else she had on the menu.

Still, it rankled. She could see it now: *Nick Avery, former chef at Le Chapeau Noir, saves struggling restaurant in the heart of the Mission District.* It would look good on a press release, she thought sourly. Or better, on a resumé.

She closed her eyes for a second and leaned her head against one of the shelves. Maybe she was just bitter. She'd taken on a lot—Lindsay often chided her for not delegating more. But the lessons she'd learned early on were difficult to unlearn. She'd tried so hard to be everything to everyone…and had wound up pleasing no one, and taking all the blame when Le Pome had failed. From then on, she took responsibility for everything.

She wasn't about to turn over her fate, and that of her restaurant, to someone she barely knew…and had almost slept with.

She heard footsteps behind her, and made a guess at who it was. "Mari, we need to talk."

She didn't open her eyes, simply sighed deeply. "Can it wait?"

"As a matter of fact," she heard Nick's voice say sternly, "it's already waited over twenty-four hours. I'd say I'm due."

She heard the pantry door shut behind him, and her head jerked up. "What are you doing?"

"Getting a moment of privacy with you," he said in a low voice, his arms crossing in front of his chest. Now that she knew what it looked like without a shirt, she forced herself to stay focused on his eyes. They were gleaming with anger—and some undefined emotion, something she couldn't quite put her finger on.

"Well, you can get a moment's privacy on break," she said, hating the fact that her voice trembled slightly. "I've got to come up with the special for the day."

"Forget the special," he said, advancing on her. "We need to talk. About Sunday night."

She shrugged. "What's to talk about? I made a mistake. *We* made a mistake. Let's just put it behind us and stay professional, shall we?" The last word ended on a high note of surprise as he backed her against a shelf, putting a strong arm on either side of her.

"Do you honestly think we can put whatever this is between us—'behind' us?" he said, in a low voice that ran over her like a caress.

She looked down at the floor. No. She'd been telling herself that she could put it aside, since the night he walked into the restaurant. She'd repeated it when she kissed him after his interview, when she'd invited him over to cook for her. Even when she'd stripped down to her underwear and writhed beneath him in her living room.

She'd been lying to herself.

She put her arms up, knocking his arms aside. "This he-man crap does nothing for me, Nick."

"How about this, then?" He put one hand on her shoulder, and another under her chin, forcing her gaze back to his eyes. "I'm not trying to pull a fast one on you. Sure, yeah, I'll be honest. It'd be great to have a few signature dishes on the menu. It'd be easier to get promotion. It'd be easier to get my name back. Is that what you want to hear?''

She didn't look away, but she swallowed hard. *No, what I want to hear is, "Mari, I want to help you, I don't care about my reputation, I just want to get you through this."* She almost laughed at her own naive desires.

She shrugged, and he let out an irritated huff.

''Did it occur to you that, since jobs aren't all that easy to come by for me right now, the fate of your restaurant is now *my* problem as well?''

She looked at him. Self-motivation…and self-preservation. She couldn't really blame him for that.

''I'll take care of it,'' she said. ''I always have.''

He stared at her, and she felt the usual warmth…with an undercurrent of wariness. Finally, he jerked his chin toward the door. ''They don't know, do they?''

Now a spike of ice hit her in the chest. ''They don't know what?''

''That you're going under. They have no idea how dire the situation is.''

''I haven't told them.'' She felt her own chin go up a notch. ''And it's not as bad as you—''

''What would they do, I wonder?'' His eyes were fixed on her like a rifle sight. ''Quit? Leave, while they still could?''

''No,'' she said instantly, angry. ''They care about me. They're loyal. I've known them for years.''

But they'd worry, she thought, with a slight edge of

panic. They were the closest thing she had to a family. That was why she hadn't told them.

That was yet one more reason she had to turn this whole thing around.

"So…it wouldn't hurt to tell them."

He let the words linger in the air for a second.

She realized the gist of what he was saying. "This is blackmail," she said flatly.

"I prefer to think of it as reasoning with someone who refuses to see reason, but you can call it what you like." His voice was firm. "I'm not saying hand over the keys, dammit. I'm just saying…let me help you."

She nudged him away from her, crossing her arms and standing in the furthest corner away from him— which, in this admittedly tiny walk-in, was not very far. "Help me how?"

"Let me cook for you. For real this time," he said, when she made a snorting sound of disbelief. "We come up with the right theme, develop the right menu, get the right people to look at it…I could help you save this place, Mari."

She closed her eyes.

What choice did she have, really?

"All right," she said. "But it doesn't get your name on it. I don't want this to become a celebrity chef thing."

He grimaced. "All right. And we work at my place."

Her eyes widened. "Why?"

He turned toward the door. "Because I'm sick of you having home court advantage. So...tonight?"

She shook her head. "After an eleven-hour shift? My brain's going to be like tapioca." She took a deep breath. "And I don't want to brainstorm in front of the crew. They'll know something's wrong if we rework the whole menu in front of them."

His eyes glowed. "All right. Then Sunday night again...and Monday morning."

NICK'S WORDS WERE STILL echoing in Mari's head on Thursday. Whenever they had a break, he had something for her to taste, usually with a "close your eyes and try this" while his fingers tickled her lips, distracting her from the taste of the food. He talked with her about possible menu items, but all she could sense was the incredible heat from his eyes.

Mari Salazar, you are losing your mind.

The phone rang, and she answered it. "Guilty Pleasures, this is Mari."

"Mari? This is Leon."

"Leon!" she said. She saw Nick's eyebrow quirk up, and she smiled at him before disappearing into the back room with the cordless. "I haven't heard from you in a while. How's it going?"

"The usual. At least here I don't have to teach first year students anymore." He chuckled. "I don't have a lot of time to talk, but I was wondering...did Nick Avery get in touch with you?"

Mari felt a slight blush heat her face. "Um, yes. I meant to call you about him."

She heard Leon let out a sigh on the other end of the line. "I hope I didn't put you too much on the spot," he said, his voice full of apology, "but if you've seen him cook at all, you'll know how incredibly talented he is."

Mari knew how talented he was. *And not all of it was his cooking.*

She blushed harder and stammered. "Well, yes…"

"He was a brilliant student. I can vouch for that." Now her old teacher had pressed into hard-sell mode, something she'd never heard him do before. "More than his talent, he's an incredibly hard worker. He's got drive…you wouldn't believe the extent of his ambitions."

Mari frowned. It was easy to overlook his ambitions when he was seducing you with a few words and a few random touches…easier still when your body was dying to be seduced. But this drove home the point.

"I can imagine just how ambitious he is," Mari said, her voice turning slightly sour.

Leon was silent for a second. "Perhaps I am misrepresenting him," he said, and she could tell the note of confusion in his accent. "I don't mean that he's unscrupulous, certainly. He just wants to be the best. And he's as close to being the best as any I've seen."

Mari let out a low breath. "Yes. I know he's talented. And I know he's a hard worker. I hired him, Leon."

She could almost feel the relief over the phone line. "Ah, that's wonderful. So? He's working out well, then?"

Mari glanced at the door, hoping he wasn't listening. "He's working out pretty well, yes."

"You sound reserved." Leon paused. "Good grief. This isn't that nonsense from Chapeau, is it?"

"No, no, of course not." The *last* thing she was thinking of was his past reputation. He could've robbed the place blind and all she'd be thinking of was how good his hands felt on her.

Definitely losing my mind.

"Then what is it?"

Mari took a deep breath, then peered out. Nick looked busy at the sauté station, so she muttered into the phone, "He's a little...er, *distracting,* isn't he?"

"Distracting?" Leon sounded puzzled. "How so?"

Mari grimaced. No, Nick definitely wasn't listening. "He's sort of a feast for the eyes, I mean."

Leon burst out laughing. "Oh. Distracting. I see."

"But he's talented, and I'm all about second chances, so don't worry there," Mari said hurriedly. "I just...I wasn't...I don't know. He wasn't what I was expecting."

"He'll work out fine," Leon said, his voice still laced with humor. "If you need help keeping him in line, you just give me a call, and I'll come and visit."

"Keeping him in line?"

Leon paused again. "Well, he's used to having his own kitchen, is all I meant. And I imagine under the circumstances—being distracted—that could become a problem?"

"Ha, ha, Leon."

He laughed again. "All right, I have to go. I just

wanted to make sure he was settled and that you were working well together.''

''Oh, we're fine. Absolutely.''

''Perfect. I'll talk to you later, Mari.''

''Bye, Leon.'' She clicked the phone off, then turned.

Nick was standing in the doorway. ''How's Leon doing?''

Was it just her, or did he have a smirk hovering at the corner of his lips?

''He's fine,'' she said with a small shrug. ''He wanted to make sure you were doing all right.''

''He's a good man.'' Nick was crowding the doorway, so there was no way Mari could walk past without brushing against him…and she now knew from experience how *distracting* that could be.

''He also said that if you were being a pain, he'd come down and straighten you out.''

Nick grinned. ''I'll keep that in mind.''

It didn't look like he was moving, so she finally walked up to him. ''You're in my way.''

He leaned down, so she could feel the brush of his breath against her neck. ''Feast for the eyes, huh?''

Mari shut her eyes, gritting her teeth. Of course he heard that one.

''Wait till Sunday,'' he said, leaning against the door frame and giving her barely enough room to walk past. ''Maybe I'll be able to come up with a feast for the rest of you.''

NICK WORKED TUESDAY through Saturday at Guilty Pleasures, watching as Mari tried her damnedest to avoid him, even though he felt her gaze on him whenever he wasn't looking. Which wasn't often, since he couldn't seem to take his eyes off of her, either. It was strange, this attraction.

He grimaced to himself. Of course, watching her fall apart under his fingertips might have something to do with it.

He walked through the stalls of a farmer's market, looking at the fresh produce…garnet-colored strawberries, lemon cucumbers, baby spinach. The smell of kettle corn and baked goods permeated the air. He was getting the ingredients for the Great Menu Experiment, as he was mentally calling it. With any luck, he'd help come up with a theme that would attract reviews and publicity, which would then in turn bring in business. Which would help his reputation.

He bought a half pound of hot chili almond brittle, thinking of how to incorporate it into a dessert. With any luck, it would garner the same reaction as the chocolate. He might be in this to help the restaurant, but he was honest enough to realize that he had an ulterior motive.

He wanted to sleep with Mari Salazar.

It had been a pure sensual pleasure to watch the woman eat. As someone whose life and obsessions revolved around food, maybe he was more attuned to it than the average man, but the way she closed her eyes to savor the flavors, and that low moan of appreciation, all were simply precursors to the way she responded to the passion between them. It had been like a sexual sneak-preview.

It had turned him on to an unbelievable extent. He was looking forward to repeating the experience…only this time, he wouldn't get kicked out after a phone call. He'd see to that.

"Hey, Nick. How's it going?"

Nick glanced over, feeling a clench in his stomach. It was Bob Blackstone, a restaurant owner from New York who had recently moved to a swank new restaurant in the city. He'd tried getting a job from Bob when Phillip had fired him, and Bob had reluctantly said no…just like everyone else Nick had interviewed with. At least he was more polite about it—Nick had interned with Bob's New York restaurant, Blackstone's, when he was at the Culinary School.

"Hey, Bob. Things are going…" He paused, thinking it over. "Well, they're going."

Bob laughed, the polite laugh of someone who's not sure how to respond. "Did you get a job yet?"

"Yeah. Sous chef, but it's got potential." At least, he was betting that there would be.

"Really?" If anything, Bob sounded relieved. Nick had liked him enough to cut him slack—it was hard to go up against a rich, established family like the Marceaus if you were in the restaurant industry. And Bob had sounded both guilty and sorry when he'd turned him down. "That's fantastic, really fantastic. Where? Henri's? Stars?"

Nick winced. "Well, I'm not sure you'll have heard of it…."

"Smaller places are good to build your reputation," Bob said, with a wave of his hand. "You let me know where, and I can start spreading buzz."

Suddenly, Nick wasn't sure if he *wanted* buzz about Mari's restaurant—at least, not until he could whip it into shape. "It's a little place in the Mission District," Nick hedged, then realizing Bob wasn't going to let up in his drive to be helpful, he sighed. "It's called Guilty Pleasures. Heard of it?"

He saw the exact moment when Bob registered the restaurant. "Oh. I think I've driven by it."

Not exactly a ringing endorsement, Nick thought.

"Well. It's good that you're working, at least, right?" Bob's tone was falsely cheerful, and Nick noticed that the offer of "building up buzz" was not repeated. "And you'll get past this. Hell, I'd offer you a job myself, only..." Bob shifted his weight nervously from foot to foot. "You understand."

"Yeah. I understand." Nick tried to keep the bitterness out of his voice, but a drop still crept in.

"Well..." Bob looked away, and Nick could tell he was sorry he'd even asked. "I've got to pick up some stuff for tomorrow. You should stop by the restaurant some time. Don't be a stranger."

Nick quirked an eyebrow at him. "Really?"

"Sure." Bob smiled genially and held out his hand. "I'll buy you dinner. See you around."

Nick shook his hand, then gritted his teeth as Bob wandered back out into the crowd of pedestrian traffic. It was all he could do not to crush the almond brittle he was holding.

It was one thing to be targeted, taunted, and humiliated, he thought. He'd put up with that all his life.

But *pitied*…

Nick gritted his teeth. He couldn't stand for that.

He started purchasing in earnest, his mind going into overdrive with possibilities. He could picture Guilty Pleasures in his head, not as the slow, third-rate restaurant it was now, but filled with people, getting four star reviews.

Getting his name out.

He purchased ingredients, his mind full of grim determination. His thoughts of Mari's sensual delights were crowded out of his mind by more pressing matters.

Lust was one thing, he thought.

Reputation…now, that was forever.

MARI SHOWED UP AT Nick's house that night around nine-forty-five. The restaurant had had virtually no business…it was the slowest she'd seen it since the first week they opened, and only drove home the fact that she had to do something, soon. She'd already mentioned in passing to Lindsay that if she wanted to get that critic in, Mari would definitely be open to the possibility.

At this point, even *bad* word of mouth was better than this slow, silent dying. The downside to all this was, she now had a combination of tense, stress-filled desperation, and an excess of nervous energy.

This was how you got in trouble with Nick the last time.

But she wasn't going to repeat last Sunday's mistake. She'd kept her work clothes on, deliberately not wearing anything that might be construed as seductive. She had her notebook with her. She got the strong feeling that he would try to seduce her again, and while part of her body was more than willing— in fact, was wanting—to let him try, her logical mind was standing at the fore today.

She wasn't going to bury her fear in sex. She was going to focus, get this menu done, and get out. That was all.

She walked up the steps that led to his front door, and knocked. After a moment, he answered. He was wearing a pair of low-slung jeans and a crisp white T-shirt that already had signs of food on it. His eyes looked unfocused.

"Good. You're here," he said. Before she could answer this greeting, he had already turned and was heading back into his house.

Oh, yeah. This guy's trying to seduce you.

Mari ignored the mocking tone of her subconscious, shutting the door and following him into his kitchen. It was larger than hers—not surprisingly—and already there were four pots bubbling away on the stove. There was also a lot of food strewn on the kitchen counters, and piled on one side of the broad oak kitchen table. On the other side, he had sketches laid out in a large notepad, with a scrawling handwriting not unlike her own. She stared, fascinated.

"How long have you been at this?"

"Huh? Oh. Since about four today," he said, going

back and stirring something in one of the pots. "I've got some ideas, but I think we've got a long way to go."

She nodded, trying to stay serious herself, even while part of her felt the tiniest bit bereft. There was none of the double-entendre of last Sunday's meal-making, she noticed... He barely seemed to register that she was there. He looked like a man possessed.

By food, that was, she thought ruefully. Not sex.

She sat down at the table. She wasn't going to be disappointed. This was what she wanted. This was what *had* to happen. "So. What ideas have you come up with so far?"

He sat down next to her, going over his drawings. He smelled like...garlic, she thought with a silent laugh. And oregano, and lemongrass, and cinnamon. All overlaying a basic male scent. It should have been disgusting, but instead it was intriguing.

He flipped over a drawing. "So far, I've come up with three main themes. There's French, of course..."

"No French," Mari said, a knee-jerk reaction. Derek, the owner of Le Pome, had insisted that French was the way to go, too. She didn't mind eating French food, but damn if she was going to cook it again.

He frowned. "It was just a start. Okay, then there's the 'light food' approach: natural fruits and vegetables, organic meats..."

She frowned, looking at the menu he'd come up with. "That's not us," she said bluntly. When he frowned back at her, she pointed out, "Going from fried foods and ice-cream sundaes one day to organic veggies and tofu shakes the next? Come on. We'd be schizophrenic. And my crew won't believe in this kind of food, I can guarantee it.''

Nick looked disgruntled. It was interesting to see him this way—not trying to charm her or seduce her, but genuinely working.

It was a bit of a turn on, actually.

She frowned down at the page he was doodling on. *What about this guy* isn't *a turn-on, though?*

''All right,'' he said. ''Now we start to get into the more artsy stuff. I've got a couple of ideas: Gypsy, with Moroccan and maybe Spanish influences; Noir, with sort of stark foods and some fifties influences; or maybe Alien, with really weird food combinations.''

She raised an eyebrow at him. *''Alien?''*

He took a deep breath. ''That's why it's called brainstorming, Mari.''

She looked over the sketches, reaching for a pencil just as he reached for the same. Her hand brushed against his, and she looked at him.

He simply shrugged and reached for a nearby pen, not acknowledging their touch, even while she felt the slight jolt from it.

''We might be able to work with the Gypsy thing,'' she said, starting to hunker down. She was focusing, getting serious. ''Let's see what menu ideas you had in mind.''

Still, she couldn't get over the lingering feeling that was haunting her. She could have sworn it was disappointment.

SEVERAL HOURS and many failed dish attempts later, she and Nick were at each other's throats. Sandy-eyed,

Mari looked over the long list of themes they'd managed to kick around. They'd moved from Gypsy and Alien to Fiesta, Fusion, Museum—with sculpted food, Pie House—a short-lived idea, and even Circus—even shorter-lived. Now, at three in the morning, Nick ran his fingers through his hair and rubbed at his eyes.

"I think we've hit a wall," he said, stating the obvious. He stretched, giving her a view of his tightly corded abs. "Maybe we should try picking it up again tomorrow."

Her mouth went dry.

Too bad we can't have a menu about sex.

The thought was so ludicrous, she wound up laughing. He looked at her with a puzzled smile.

"What?"

She was too tired to come up with a proper lie. "I was just thinking…there's one theme we haven't hit on. Sex."

He blinked, and she laughed even harder. "Sex, huh?" he finally said. "Well. It can't be worse than Circus."

She was chuckling in deep, hitching breaths now. "Can't you see it? We could call the appetizers Foreplay or something."

He leaned next to her, and brushed her shoulder. Suddenly, a good deal of her tiredness fled in the face of a wave of desire that hit her like a slap. Apparently the better part of her restraint and a good deal of her common sense had already gone to sleep.

Now, there was just wanting—and Nick.

Nick smiled, oblivious to the change that had just occurred in Mari. ''Hmm. Foreplay. Could work. We could offer oysters, artichoke hearts…potential aphrodisiac stuff like that. Have drinks like Spanish Fly and Blowjobs.'' He chuckled to himself.

She leaned forward, scooting her chair closer to his. ''I could be on to something,'' she purred. ''You'd go from Foreplay to Main Intercourses.''

Nick snickered, until he noticed how close she was. Then his laughter stopped, and his eyes glowed. She noticed the vein at the base of his neck pulsing as she stroked one of his legs with a barely-there touch of her fingertips.

''We'd need to come up with a variety of stuff,'' she said, her voice coaxing. ''You don't want the same thing all the time.''

''Of course not,'' he said, his breathing a little ragged. ''So…sexy main dishes.''

''Intercourses,'' she murmured, and he closed his eyes slightly as she reached his thigh, only brushing toward the juncture before moving back to his knees. She watched as he bunched his hands into fists.

''Are you sure this is a good idea?'' he said, his eyes golden and glowing.

No, she wasn't. More importantly, she didn't care. She continued onward, implacably. ''I was thinking of splitting it into a few sub menus… Quickies, for people who don't have a lot of time, for example. Big Meat,'' and now her hand started heading north again, eliciting a low groan from Nick. ''For those who like that sort of thing. Exotic and Spicy menus for people who want their intercourse different and…*hot.*''

He leaned back, and she traced the erection that was straining against the fly of his jeans. ''And which are you?'' he asked in a strangled whisper.

''I think we can come up with the Quickie menu later,'' she said, unbuttoning his jeans and tugging the zipper down slowly, a tooth at a time. ''But the rest of them…the Spicy, the Exotic, the *Big Meat*…'' She smiled as she freed his cock from the restraints of denim and cotton, as Nick gripped the sides of the chair as if he would break the wood with his bare hands. ''I think I'd like to try a little of each tonight. If you're up to it.''

He didn't open his eyes, and he was breathing in slow, sharp panting breaths. ''I think you can tell that I'm up to it.''

She knelt down in between his legs, her lips brushing against his hardness. ''Well then. I think I'll start with a taste test.'' With that, she took him into her mouth as he gasped and then let out a low moan.

He tasted tangy, she noted as she brushed against his erection with her tongue, teasing the smooth skin of his head and lightly, very lightly, dragging her teeth down the delicate skin of his shaft. She relished the sound of him, the feel of his thigh muscles bunching as she dragged her nails down the denim of his jeans. He lifted his hips slightly off the chair as she increased suction, treating him like some new delicacy that she devoured with loving licks.

Finally, he tugged her up. ''I need to be inside

you,'' he said. His eyes were an inferno of desire. *''Now.''*

She stood up, almost laughing at the way he looked with his cock standing stiffly from his unzipped jeans and opened boxers. ''Well, we've had the big meat,'' she said, tongue firmly in cheek even as she felt a rush of wetness between her legs. She wasn't tired any more. She was just *hot.* ''Think you can get me to Spicy or Exotic?''

He smiled with sensual promise. ''I think I can come up with something.''

He swung her up in his arms, causing her to laugh. Then he took her to his bedroom. It was neat, and utterly masculine…much different from the gauzy femininity of her own bed. He placed her on the comforter of his bed…it might be plain, but it was soft, and luxuriously comfortable. She watched as he shucked his shirt, pants and boxers off, sucking in her breath as she finally saw him in all his naked glory. He wasn't the slightest bit self-conscious.

''Let's start with exotic, shall we?''

She felt heat pierce her from between her legs to the pit of her stomach, and her breasts tingled. ''Why don't we?''

''Take off your clothes,'' he ordered.

She raised an eyebrow, but he turned to one of his drawers. ''What are *you* going to be doing?'' she asked, peeling off her shirt and pants.

He removed a small box. ''Getting to the exotic, as Mademoiselle requested.''

She smiled, but she could feel her pulse pounding

in her chest. She took off her bra and panties, and felt the smooth weave of the comforter beneath her back and against her bottom. She leaned on one side, smiling seductively.

"So. What do you have for me?"

He took out a small pot of what looked like powder. She frowned at it. "What's that?"

"Try it," he said, putting his finger in and licking it. She followed suit, then smiled.

"What *is* that?"

"Honey dust," he said, his eyes like a sorcerer's. "Now just lie still."

She did as requested, intrigued. He produced what looked like a tiny bundle of feathers, dusting her body with soft, ticklish, torturing strokes. It was as if he were waking up every nerve ending she had with a tiny brush of the feathers. By the time he was done, she was throbbing with need.

"Now, you'll see why it's honey dust," he said with a grin. And he proceeded to lick the dust from her body.

She groaned and writhed beneath his searching lips, the heat and warmth of his mouth and tongue massaging her arms, her shoulders, her neck. He pressed heated kisses against her thighs and the backs of her knees. She almost cried with the unknown pleasure of it. She'd enjoyed sex before, but this…it was as if all the others had been bungling amateurs, as if she herself hadn't really realized what sex could be. She felt awed by it.

When he was finished, she was damp with her own

desire and trembling against the comforter, shivering with sexual heat. "Come inside me," she said, spreading her legs slightly. "Please."

He grinned, and she noticed a fine trembling in his skin, as well. "We haven't even gotten to spicy yet," he said, "But I don't think I can wait."

He went back to the drawer, and got out a bunch of condoms. "Don't suppose you have a flavor preference," he said, with a low, rasping laugh.

She sat up at that one, glancing at the selection. Wild cherry, strawberry, mango. She laughed. "We'll have to add these to the menu," she said, plucking the wild cherry package out of his hand. Then she tugged him down to the bed. His skin felt like hot satin. "Allow me."

She put the condom over the tip of him, then rolled it the rest of the way with her mouth. True to the company's word, the condom *did* taste like cherry. She giggled.

Then he rolled on top of her, and all laughter stopped. The shock of his skin on top of hers made her moan as the sensitive flesh of her skin clenched in anticipation. "Nick," she whispered.

He reached down, stroking her breasts, nuzzling her neck…then positioned himself between her legs, stroking his cock against the soft skin of her thighs. She spread herself invitingly.

He pressed in by inches, brushing against her clitoris as he made his entry. She closed her eyes against the sensation as her back arched to accept him. When he'd pressed himself fully into her, she felt stretched. The sensation was fantastic.

"Mari," he breathed, and began to move, his hips slowly withdrawing and then pressing against her, causing a slow cascade of sensation to wash over her. When she raised her legs to take even more of him in, he clutched one of her legs high over his hip, causing him to position his cock directly onto her G-spot.

She moaned, and bucked against him. He increased his speed, still smooth but firm as he pressed against her relentlessly. She pushed up to meet him, the joining of the base of his shaft against her clitoris enough to make her cry out. "Oh...oh, yes..." She dragged her nails against his back, and he moaned low, now moving against her faster.

She felt the first tremors of orgasm start with a clutching of her muscles, and suddenly it was like an explosion of warmth, circulating from her sex to the rest of her body in a tidal wave. She let out a loud cry, clenching against him.

His body responded with one last strong drive, and he groaned in response as his orgasm hit, pulsing against her as he pressed into her a few more gentle times, as if he couldn't get deep enough into her.

She felt deliciously limp and boneless as he collapsed against her. Their sweat-slick bodies slid against each other, and she smiled.

"I think that's the best idea we've had all night," she said, the satisfaction of her body coming through in her words.

He rolled off of her, taking care of the condom

before moving back to her side, brushing the hair out of her face and smiling. She thought that the sex had surprised her, but now she was even more shocked to find the tenderness of his gaze and of the gentle caressing strokes of his fingertips.

"Downright brilliant," he said, and she knew he felt the same way.

Without really thinking about it, she leaned up and kissed him...a gentle, non-seductive kiss. Of gratitude, maybe. Or just because he was looking at her as if he cared.

When she leaned back down, she felt embarrassed. The bizarre attraction between them was powerful, but it was lust. What she was feeling now—this tenderness—really didn't have a place in it. She bit her lip, waiting for his reaction, if there was one.

He didn't seem to notice, but instead kissed her back, causing her chest to tighten with unwise happiness. "You know, I really do think you're onto something."

She laughed. "Well, we'll just have to try again tomorrow," she said, stroking his naked body and trying to keep her heart out of it. "After we work on the menu some more."

"No," he said, stroking her back. "I meant, you might be on to something with the menu."

She laughed until she realized—he was serious. "Nick, I don't know if you realize this, but I was trying to jump you." She shook her head. "You can't put this stuff on a menu!"

"Well, not as is, but think about it. You've got a

restaurant called Guilty Pleasures. It's got a sexual connotation already, sort of.''

She laughed, this time more nervously. "I can't believe I'm hearing this."

"I mean it," he said, his voice coaxing. "Foreplay for appetizers, Main Intercourses, Afterglow for dessert. You've got the submenus."

"I was kidding around," she interrupted.

"But it *works*. And we could come up with some killer ideas. It'd be a shoo-in for publicity. People would love it. It would be original."

She rolled onto her back. It could work...but did she want it to? "I don't know, Nick. It's awfully weird. I don't want to become the Porn Queen of the restaurant world."

He laughed. "The dishes would make the difference. It wouldn't be obscene. We could make it beautiful."

She looked at him. He was serious...and the look in his eyes was determined. He had latched onto something.

And the thing was, he *had* taken a blazing sexual experience and turned it into something artistic—and beautiful.

"Let's give it a try," she said, softly.

He smiled. "Believe me," he said, kissing her again with more intent. "We will."

4

ONE MONTH LATER, Nick stood in the kitchen of Guilty Pleasures. Tonight, they were rolling out the new menu…the new *sexy* menu. And he knew deep in his heart that, unconventional as it was, it was going to *work*.

Now if he could just convince Mari of that fact.

He and Mari had worked very closely on the menu together—closer than the crew or Lindsay had suspected. They'd personally tried out a lot of variations on the menu, and on each other. He remembered the previous night with particular fondness, standing in his shower, letting the warm water wash over both of their bodies as he entered her and brought her to climax.

He closed his eyes. He seemed to be at a state of semi-erection whenever he thought about Mari—and it seemed like he'd thought about Mari every moment of every day for the past month.

It made the menu very authentic, he thought with a rueful grin. If the crew suspected just how intimately he worked with Mari, they kept it to themselves. As for Mari, she never made any overt actions toward Nick while they were in the kitchen. Their relationship there was strictly professional. Still, if the two of them happened to be alone for a moment in the walk-in or the back office, he couldn't resist pressing a kiss at the nape of her neck, or half-closing his eyes as she brushed against his body with a smile of promise and disappeared.

No wonder I'm in a perpetual state of semi-hard. He imagined his body would get used to it—especially if he stayed at Guilty Pleasures for any length of time.

That produced a frown. He was still intent on getting his reputation back, and being a chef at a four-star restaurant… Hell, preferably his *own* four-star restaurant. But for the meantime, there was nowhere else he'd rather be while trying to rebuild his reputation. And this sexual extravaganza would probably at least get him some attention. It was a risk he was willing to take.

He looked over to where Mari was supervising the line cooks as they made the new dishes: b'ystella, coq au vin, the oysters and the "eight-inch bangers." Tiny was letting out his booming laugh.

"Well, it may be a damned foolish thing," Tiny said as he grilled up the Spicy Hot Beefcakes, "but it's a hell of a lot of fun."

Mari smiled nervously.

It was a risk, Nick realized…and not just to his reputation. Mari needed a financial windfall. She was the one with the most to lose.

He walked up to her. "You okay?" he whispered.

She nudged him away. "I'll be fine," she said, wearing what he had come to call her "seasoned pro" face. With all their gibes and their comments, he was surprised none of the crew, who had known Mari so much longer than he himself had, could tell just how wound up she was. She might be wearing a bright smile, but he could sense it coming off her in waves— could see it in the tensing of her shoulders, in the short, sharp movements that replaced her usual fluid grace.

She wouldn't be all right, he realized, until this night was over. Then, he'd make sure that she felt all right...when he had her safely tucked into his bed, and he could work on relaxing her properly.

He realized he wanted very badly to help her feel better.

"All right. Customers are here. Let's see what their reaction to the new menu is," Mari said, and Nick saw her tense up, like a mouse sensing a cat. The rest of the crew peered out the window with her, looking at the few stragglers of customers that had made their way in, drawn by the "New Menu!" banner they'd hung out front.

The people sat down, getting their menus, and Nick could barely make out the flurry of their conversation. They were obviously surprised. Then one of the men of the group burst out into laughter, which his companions joined in with.

"I guess that means they like it?" Zooey, the youngster of the group, said nervously.

Mari shrugged. "Well, they're not leaving."

The waitress took the table's order, and brought the ticket back with a broad smile. "They're ordering the whole shebang…several appetizers—I'm sorry, *Fore-plays*—two beefcakes, one coq au vin, one Holy Molé. And they've already said they're going to order dessert. They've even ordered drinks!''

The crew let out a cheer before going back to their respective stations. Nick watched as Mari let out a slow breath, and her shoulders relaxed slightly. ''All right, now it's up to us,'' she said, in her commander's voice. ''Let's make sure they come back.''

The waitress pulled Nick and Mari aside. ''They were getting on their cell phones and calling some friends,'' she confided, with a grin. ''I think we're going to do well!''

Mari smiled at this one. ''Let's hope so. Make sure they get their drinks,'' Mari said, then turned to Nick. ''This looks promising.''

Nick noticed that none of the crew was paying attention, and he leaned down to whisper in her ear. ''If this takes off, I'm going to want to celebrate with you properly…and maybe work on some specials.''

He watched as her eyes darted nervously to the other people in the kitchen, but no one else noticed their conversation. ''Not here, Nick,'' she said, her voice faintly chiding…and still, he could hear the tone of arousal in her voice.

He grinned and got to work.

The restaurant *was* busier. Apparently there was a party going on in a loft down the street—a sort of rave—and the word of mouth of the patrons was spreading to all the friends who'd planned to attend. The kitchen crew was jumping all evening. They must have plated up over a hundred meals. By the end of the evening, the crew was dead on its feet, and several of them had to insist that several patrons leave so they could close.

Nick leaned next to Mari, watching as the crew dragged their way through the cleaning and closing checklist. "I think we did it," he said, rubbing at his sore neck.

She smiled. "Guess we ought to work on those specials, then," she whispered back.

He turned to her, but before he could respond, Lindsay came in. Mari's eyes widened as she looked at her watch. "Hi, there. What are you doing here? I wasn't expecting to see you till tomorrow…"

"This? This was your new menu?" Lindsay said, without preamble.

Mari blinked. "I know you've been out of town," she said slowly, "but I told you about the concept…."

"I thought you said that the dishes were *sensual*," Lindsay said, all but ignoring Nick. "Not…not *porn!*"

Mari flinched, and Nick stepped in. "They're not porn," he said sharply. "Risqué, maybe…"

"'Foreplays'? 'Intercourses'? 'Afterglow'?" Lindsay's voice was incredulous. "And *'cock au vin,'* for pity's sake? What are you trying to do?"

"What's the problem, Lindsay?" Mari finally said, crossing her arms. The crew had stopped in their cleanup efforts, and were listening to the confrontation intently. "It's not that big a deal."

"Starting a new menu is a big deal from a publicity

standpoint,'' Lindsay said. "God, Mari, I invited critics tonight."

Nick saw Mari's shoulders draw together, as if the
bands of muscles tightened to the point of snapping.
"Well, so what? Even if the publicity's bad, I could
use some local press coverage. And the people who
read between the lines…"

"*I invited the* San Francisco Food & Wine *editor
here tonight,*" Lindsay said in a sharp tone of voice.
"I invited the food critics from the *Chronicle,* yes, as
well as the *Guardian* and the *Weekly.* I even invited
the Galloping Gourmet from channel four news!
That's why I'm upset. Don't you see? They could
bury us!"

Whenever he'd seen Mari's friend, she had always
seemed to be the opposite of Mari…cool where Mari
was hot, buttoned up where Mari was flagrant. Now,
he saw that calm exterior crack.

"Mari, I think I've made a terrible mistake." Lindsay said, her voice trembling. "I think *we've* made a
terrible mistake."

He watched as Mari tugged Lindsay over to the
back room, and he followed, sensing the eyes of the
crew on his back. "Lindsay, it's not that bad," Mari
said, her voice like steel. "We'll make it through. It
can't be worse, right?"

Lindsay's eyes were sorrowful. "But…I remember
last time…" Lindsay said, her voice apologetic. "I
know you didn't want this to happen again."

Nick frowned. *Again?* What was she talking about?

As far as he knew, Guilty Pleasures had gotten *no* previous coverage from the food press.

Still, the tension coming from Mari was palpable. ''You were doing what you felt was best for the restaurant. And so was I, Lindsay,'' she said, in a low voice. Mari hugged Lindsay, and to his surprise, Lindsay hugged back. ''We'll do fine.''

''Sorry. I didn't mean to fly off the handle like that,'' Lindsay responded, her voice uneven. ''I'm sure we'll be fine.''

''Go on home. I'll talk to you tomorrow.''

Lindsay nodded, and walked out the door, barely giving Nick a glance. Nick stayed focused on Mari. ''It will be all right,'' he said, although from the picture Lindsay painted, there was good potential that it was going to sting like hell. He would have wanted to get the kinks worked out of the new menu before getting press…right now it was a crap-shoot, and things could go either way.

Mari shrugged, but her eyes were dark, looking like deep violet storm clouds.

He sighed, and reached for her, then frowned when she pulled away, looking at the door. ''What did she mean, by the way?'' Nick asked, trying not to be disturbed by the fact that she didn't want him touching her with her crew nearby.

''Hmm?'' Mari's voice was listless.

''By what happened before. What was she talking about?''

That woke Mari out of her lethargy. Her eyes snapped to his.

"It doesn't matter," she said firmly, leading him to believe that it mattered, a lot. "You can go home, if you want. I'll lock up."

He looked at her, and heard what she wasn't saying. *Go home. I'm not coming with you.*

"Mari," he protested, and she held up her hands.

"Nick, I need to process this," she said. "It might be nothing. On the other hand, it might be a disaster. We won't know till the articles start coming out." She laughed, but it was a flat laugh. "I am not going to be good company, if you get my point."

He sighed roughly. "I don't need you to be good company," he said in a low voice. "I want to help you feel better."

"That's nice," she said, and she was placating him. He knew that. "But this is my problem."

That pricked at his anger. "You're not the only one with something at stake here," he reminded her.

She looked at him, and he saw a responding anger alight in her eyes. "Really? What are *you* risking, Nick? The chance to become a four-star chef and get your fame and your rep back?" Her voice was brimming with disdain. "Sooner or later, it'll get through that thick skull of yours that you can get a job in another city. Or in another country. *You're that good, Nick.*"

He stared at her, his mouth agape. She spoke with fury, it was cold and controlled.

"But this *is* my second chance. I don't know if I'll get another one." She shrugged. "When this place goes under, you'll still be climbing the ladder and looking for glory while I'm line cooking in somebody else's kitchen.''

He watched as the pain of her words etched itself into her face. "Mari," he breathed.

She waved a hand. "Just go home, Nick." She turned away from him. "I think I'm done letting you play with me for awhile."

He waited for her to turn back.

She didn't. And after long moments, he realized she wouldn't.

"READY ON SEVEN!" Mari called. "Order up!"

Mari slid the plate of hot and spicy Honey Curry chicken onto the service window ledge. Kate, one of her waitresses, picked up the plates that were lined up there with deft skill. They were busier, that was definite, especially for lunch on a Wednesday. They weren't at a comfortable financial level yet, but soon, she hoped.

If the damned reviews don't sink us first.

She turned back to the next order ticket, fluttering on the board, and focused with Zenlike concentration. She made up three more orders and helped Paulo, who was getting overrun with orders from the sauté station. It wasn't until the next time she had a lull that she allowed herself to think about what was happening.

There hadn't been any bad reviews...yet. There hadn't been any reviews at *all*.

But the *Weekly* came out today, and the *Guardian* tomorrow...and the magazines probably a few months down the line. The newspapers would be the start.

She peered out to where the customers were laughing and eating in the front of the restaurant. It looked heartening. She wasn't going to stress about what the critics might write yet.

Yet.

She reached for another order at the same time Nick did. Their hands touched, his covering hers.

"Sorry," he said gruffly, then moved away.

Sorry. Yeah, so was she. On several levels.

She didn't regret starting the new menu, and she wasn't sorry for sleeping with him. But sleeping with him was one thing—trusting him, now that was something else.

He's a good guy, at heart, she thought to herself. *But I shouldn't have listened to him.*

The bottom line was, he was looking to make his name. He came from another world—one where *avant garde* recipes were the norm, where he had a Union Square location and a high priced menu, lots of good buzz. He could have served pickled octopus with rocks or something similar, and still have gotten away with it.

She was a small, struggling restaurant owner in a bad part of the Mission District, not that there were a lot of good parts. She wasn't trying to regain her reputation—she was trying to keep a struggling business alive. But she'd been so sex-sated, so high on her secret affair with Nick, that she hadn't listened to reason. She'd just dreamed and trusted and reveled in the sexual feast that he offered.

Well, now she was picking up the tab.

She hadn't slept with him or been alone with him since that night. She wasn't trying to punish him— she was just trying to get some distance and clear her head. He hadn't pressed her. In fact, he'd left her alone. He hadn't been cold to her, but he'd obviously been hurt, and that she regretted most of all.

It wasn't his fault, really. He had big dreams and bigger ambitions. The problem was that she needed to be more reasonable. She needed to pay attention to the big picture.

If his ambitions were to be believed, then his big picture didn't include her. Guilty Pleasures was a way station for a guy like Nick Avery. She couldn't trust her future to a guy who was looking for a way out.

Still, she thought, as she caught him looking in her direction, if it could have worked out some other way, she wished for a second that it would.

She shook her head. She was too old to believe in fairy tales.

Lindsay entered the kitchen with a dramatic push of the doors, Mo hot on her heels. Before Mari could even call out a greeting, Lindsay shook out a large newspaper.

''We're in it,'' she said, and you could have heard a pin drop in the kitchen as everybody's head spun around.

Mari shot a quick glance at Nick, who was already looking at her. She chose instead to focus on Lindsay.

No matter what happens, it was my choice, and my fault, Mari thought, steeling herself. She wasn't going to blame Nick if they got grilled.

She remembered being blamed for the failure of Le Pome. She wasn't going to have anybody else take the rap for what happened. If her restaurant was going under, then she'd take responsibility.

Lindsay opened the paper with shaking hands, and Mari gritted her teeth.

"'Treat yourself to a Guilty Pleasure,'" Lindsay started, and Mo made a triumphant thumbs-up gesture behind her back. "'Hidden in one of the roughest neighborhoods in the Mission District, a stone's throw away from an adult theater and other dens of iniquity, you'll find a garden of sinfully delicious, hilariously sexy culinary delights that will have you canceling your previous plans and heading straight home to bed...*if you're lucky*.'"

The crew, as one, cheered...and Mari felt relief wash over her like a cool bath.

Lindsay read out the rest of the review. It had some pithy things to say about the location, but overall the piece was glowing, a real boost. Mo already talked about having it framed, or maybe blown up large and put out front by the host's podium. The crew was chattering excitedly to each other.

"So, we're going to be, like, really busy from now on, huh?" Zooey said.

Paulo nudged her. "We're gonna be *money*," he said, rubbing his hands together enthusiastically.

"It's just one review," Mari said, even though some part of her felt like singing. "But good job, guys. We earned that one."

Again, they cheered, then clattered with buoyant energy through the next round of orders.

Lindsay walked up to her as Mo returned to his station. "I'm sorry," she said, tugging Mari into the back room and giving her a hug. "I shouldn't have snapped at you. Obviously I underestimated what you're capable of."

"Nick helped," Mari said. Just because she wouldn't throw the blame on him didn't mean she'd hog all the credit now that they were coming up roses. "We worked on it together."

A picture of the last time they'd *worked on it* flashed through her mind...warm water sluicing over hot bodies. She closed her eyes, suppressed a shudder.

What was he thinking now?

"All the same," Lindsay said, not noticing Mari's little sojourn down memory lane. "You did a great job, and it will do wonders for the menu. I'm sorry. I guess I just focused too much on the bottom line."

Mari patted Lindsay on the shoulder. "That's your job, remember?"

Lindsay groaned. "Job. That reminds me...I've got to see my parents. They're thinking of opening another restaurant, and they want me to go over their books."

"All right. We'll talk tomorrow."

Lindsay nodded, leaving the paper on the desk, and hurried out. Mari stayed behind, all but collapsing against the desktop as she read through the review again.

They liked it. They really liked it.

"You okay?"

It was Nick. She sensed him even before he spoke. She looked at him. "I owe you an apology."

He didn't disagree with her, just studied her with his dark golden wizard's eyes.

"I should have given our menu more of a chance," she said, shrugging. "I guess I just got scared."

He quirked one eyebrow at her. "And that's all you're apologizing for?"

She felt a small burst of irritation. "What else should I..." She thought about it, then whispered, "What? I should be sorry I didn't sleep with you while I was worried?"

Now he glanced out the door, then walked up to her. "I don't care about the sex," he said, surprising her. "What I mean is, you shut me out. You didn't have to be scared by yourself. I was a little nervous, too."

Now she gaped. "Nervous? You?"

He grinned. "I've got a good game face. But yeah, Mari, I get nervous." He paused. "And the fact that you thought I was just in it for the possible career advancement and the plentiful nooky was a trifle insulting, too, don't you think?"

She blushed. "Okay, that was uncalled for. I am really sorry about that."

He leaned close to her ear, his breath tickling the delicate skin just behind her right lobe. "Enough to make it up to me?"

She smiled, her body reacting even before she could mouth the words. "What did you have in mind?"

''I told you I wanted to celebrate, before all this happened,'' he murmured. ''And work on some specials.''

She felt heat pulse through her, and an aching between her legs. After a month of sensual exploration with this man, even a week without seemed too long.

Maybe this isn't a good idea, her subconscious stated, waving a red flag.

But in the face of her body's urging, she ignored the warning. ''What time?'' she asked instead.

NICK WAITED UNTIL every last crew member left for the night before accompanying Mari back to her apartment. It had taken some time—they had been jubilant over their first promising review, and they wanted to take Mari out for drinks to their favorite hangout, a bar called Tiger, just blocks away. Mari's gentle evasion finally worked, and now he was alone with her, headed for her loft.

It had only been a week since he'd slept with her, but his body craved hers, and the withdrawal had bordered on painful. He'd never really felt this way about sex before—he enjoyed it, naturally, but when women made demands he found it easy enough to forgo the act in order to get rid of the hassle. Besides, sex with one woman versus the other was pretty much the same.

That wasn't the case any more. He wasn't sure what made it different, but he did know that it was.

He climbed the flights of stairs to her apartment, watching as her long legs shifted and her derriere taunted him. Tonight wasn't going to just be about sex, though.

Tonight, he was going to get her to trust him.

She let him into the darkened loft, then shut and locked the door behind him. Then she reached for him, kissing him hungrily. At first, his body responded like a man dying of thirst, drinking in her lips as his hands roamed over her body. Her hands moved quickly, reaching for his pants, tugging at his shirt.

When she got his zipper down, he forced himself to back off, take some calming breaths. "Not like this, Mari."

In the dim light, he saw that her eyes were wide with surprise. "Why not?"

"Let's go to your bed," he said instead. "I want to try something."

She smiled, a small, coy smile. "Okay."

He followed her up the ladder to her bedroom. Most of the time they'd slept together had been at his house, so he took in the surroundings. She had a four-poster bed, piled high with a mountain of pillows in a pale peach color. There was a filmy white canopy that made the whole thing seem dreamlike. She sat down on the bed, still smiling.

"What did you have in mind?"

"I thought we'd talk a bit first," he said, trying hard to put a leash on his desire.

"Talk." She seemed to think about it. "Okay, let's talk."

He took a deep breath. At least she was cooperating…

She stood up and started to tug off her shirt. "You don't mind if I get comfortable while we...talk?"

He shook his head, and she pulled her shirt off slowly, revealing a pink bra edged in lace that pushed the globes of her breast up, taunting him.

"So what did you want to talk about?" she said casually, as she unbuttoned her jeans and stared at him.

He felt his pulse accelerate like with a hit of adrenaline. His mouth watered. "I wanted to talk to you about last week."

She nodded, unzipping her pants slowly and then inched them down her thighs, revealing a matching set of panties, tiny wisps of pink silk. "Okay."

It was getting hard for him to focus. It was getting hard, *period*. He fought doggedly to keep talking. This was too important to ignore.

"Do you trust me?"

She'd just kicked off her jeans, but now she froze like a startled deer, sitting on the edge of her bed in her enticing outfit. "What?"

He sat down on the edge of the bed, careful to leave some space between them. "Do you *trust* me?"

Her eyes narrowed suspiciously. "Do we have to talk about this now?"

"Mari, it hurt when you didn't come to me. When you made it seem like if anything bad happened, it was just happening to *you*." He kept his voice low and steady, but the pain of that incident still lashed at him. "I know you don't think I have as much to lose as you do...and you're right. But the fact of the matter is, I care what happens to you. If you're hurting, you don't have to be alone.''

She looked away, biting her lip unconsciously. ''Okay. Can't we just…''

''I wanted to try something different tonight.''

She looked back at him, and he swore he saw relief in her face. ''What'd you have in mind?''

''Do you mind if I look around a little bit?''

She nodded, relief sliding into puzzlement.

He rummaged through the drawers of her small dresser, feeling a shock of erotic awareness as he saw the wide variety of lingerie the woman owned. Finally, he got to what he was looking for. ''I thought so. Artistic types always have scarves.'' He pulled out three.

Now her expression turned wary. ''What do you plan to do with those?''

''Lie back.''

She stood up instead. ''I'm not so sure…''

''Mari, you've got this need to be in control. You might not always be on top, but you're always in charge. You want everything to be your call. You don't want anybody's help.'' He stroked her skin, kissing her lightly, keeping his hunger in check. ''I want to show you that sometimes, it's good to just let go, let somebody else take care of things.''

She looked away. ''I've let you…er, *take care of things.*''

He thought back to the first night, on her couch, when he'd brought her to orgasm. ''Yeah, but it was your idea. You jumped me first.''

She giggled at that one. "And I'd do it again."

"Just lie back," he said persuasively. "I'm not going to do anything you don't like. I promise."

For a second, when her gaze slid to his, she looked vulnerable…much less the tough restaurant owner she tried to project. She looked young.

"All right, Nick." She went to the bed and stretched out. "What do you want me to do?"

He smiled. "Just relax. I'll take care of the rest."

He noticed that her body was still tense…probably both with desire and nerves. He'd take care of both in a minute. First, he kissed her, keeping things gentle, brushing over her skin like a cloud. He smiled as she let out a small sound of appreciation. Then he unclasped her breasts from their restraint, licking at her raspberry-colored nipples, then sucking in slow, sure strokes. She moaned, arching up to meet him.

"Ah," he said, his voice playful. "You're helping."

"Well, I can't help it," she said.

"Lean back."

She did what he asked, and he reached for the scarves.

"First, I'm going to blindfold you," he said, wrapping a rose-colored scarf like a bandana. She sat up enough to accommodate him. He noticed that her pulse was beating rapidly in the vein in her neck. "Now, put your arms up."

Slowly, she followed his instruction.

He tied her wrists in gentle loops around the posts

of her bed. Not tight, not in any way painful…just enough to keep her from participating.

"Nick," she said, nervously.

"If you want to be untied, just say so. If there's anything uncomfortable, just let me know," he said, reassuring her. "But I'd appreciate it if you gave this a chance."

She lay there, silent. Then she nodded.

He didn't want her to feel forced or uncomfortable, and for a moment, he felt a jolt of nerves shoot through him. He was just trying to help. Was this wrong?

He shook his head. At least he'd try. And he'd stop whenever she wanted.

He tugged off his own clothes and got on the bed. She must have heard the clothes hitting the floor, because she finally smiled. "What, you strip and I can't even watch?" she joked.

He was proud of her, he thought. She *was* a tough woman, in any situation. "Just relax," he breathed, easing her panties down her legs.

"Easy for you to say," she muttered in response.

He grinned at that. Then he moved to her breasts again, teasing them with his lips and tongue. Slowly, the tension in her melted, and she began trembling and making low sounds of passion deep in her throat. He was between her legs, and she tried arching her hips to meet his erection, but he stopped her.

"See? You always want things to go at your speed," he said, with a small laugh. "Just let me worry about it."

''You're taking too long,'' she protested.

He chuckled. ''Sometimes rushing's not the answer.'' He looked down at the dark thatch of hair between her legs. ''Allow me to demonstrate.''

He moved down between her legs, and heard her breath hitch. He pressed suckling kisses on her thighs, knowing from their honey-dust experience just how sensitive her legs were. She moaned and jerked her body slightly. Then he traced the lips of her sex with his finger, feeling the rush of wetness as he saw her nipples grow peaked and taut. He dipped in slightly, feeling her warmth, and she raised herself against him.

He smiled, then leaned down and, parting her with his fingers, tasted her.

She let out a small cry, then breathed in low, panting breaths. ''Oh, *Nick*.''

He teased her clitoris with his tongue, tasting her feminine response. He nipped at her gently with his teeth, still pressing into her with one finger in slow, sure strokes. She gasped now, and heat came off of her in waves. He started sucking on her, dipping his tongue into her, replacing his finger. He stroked the soft skin of her buttocks and thighs as his mouth moved against her, in a deep, passionate kiss.

He could feel the beginnings of her orgasm, in the wave of wetness that came off her, and in the clenching of her muscles. ''Nick…Nick…'' she chanted, her hips pressing against him as he continued his relentless assault. Then he felt it, as she let out a rippling cry and convulsed against his lips.

He leaned back, kissing her legs, letting her get her

bearings. "See?" He tried not to sound smug, but the look of her pale skin with the blush of sex against it was enough to make him proud…and twice as hard, if possible. "That wasn't so bad."

"Nick," she murmured, her body still trembling lightly. "Am I allowed to ask for something?"

"Sure," he said.

"I want to feel your cock inside me. Deep."

The words rocked him like a right hook. "I think I can manage that," he finally responded in a choked voice. Hastily, he reached for his jeans, grabbing a condom out of the back pocket. He sheathed himself, then positioned himself against her again, feeling the slickness of her earlier orgasm as he slid in. He shuddered as her warmth enveloped him.

"Deep," she sighed. "Deeper."

He watched as she leaned back blindly against her pillows, her head lolling as she tried to lift her hips.

"Tell me if this is uncomfortable," he said, as he took her legs and positioned them against his shoulders. The angle made him groan as she brushed against his erection, allowing him deeper access.

"No. That's good," she breathed. "So good…"

He started moving against her, the sensation of pressing into her and withdrawing torturing them both. She was moaning against him, joining the sounds he was making as their bodies met and meshed. He pressed deeper inside her, and she moved against him, her buttocks brushing against his knees as his penis penetrated her.

"Mari," he said, his speed picking up, his body starting to move wildly toward release.

"Nick, hurry," she breathed, and she matched him stroke for stroke.

When his orgasm hit him, she let out a cry and he could feel her muscles clench with an orgasm of her own against his erection, causing even more sensation. He buried himself in her, moving against her spasmodically, almost blacking out with the intensity of sensations.

He put her legs back to either side of his body and collapsed against her, leaning up to kiss her sweat-soaked neck. "You are amazing," he whispered.

"You're...pretty amazing...yourself," she said breathlessly.

He tugged off the scarves restraining her wrists, then took off her blindfold. "Thanks," he said, stroking her face.

"For what?"

"For letting me do that," he said, shrugging. "For trusting me."

She smiled, one of the sweetest smiles he'd ever seen in his life. "I do trust you, Nick," she said in a quiet voice. "I'm just not used to leaning on anybody that way. And I guess I don't want to get used to leaning on you."

"I'm not going anywhere," he said, kissing her shoulder.

She looked at him. "Not yet, anyway."

He closed his eyes. *Not yet, anyway.*

He was going to leave, he realized. He wanted to

have his own restaurant, and as wonderful as Mari was, and as promising as he felt Guilty Pleasures could become, the fact remained...he swore he wouldn't be working in someone else's kitchen. When he'd been young, broke, and at the Culinary School on a scholarship, he promised himself that he'd be the most successful chef in the United States, with his own menu, his own staff, his own space. He'd come close to that until Phillip pulled the rug out from under him.

Now, he wanted Mari to trust him. He wanted to take care of her. But if he stayed to do that, what would happen to his dreams?

He realized she was kissing him, and he opened his eyes...only to find her positioning his wrists against the posts of her bed. She held the scarves, and her eyes gleamed with mischief.

"Do you trust me?" she said against his lips.

He smiled, and let her tie him up, feeling himself growing hard yet again, to his shock. "I trust you," he said, and he meant it.

"Good," she said, as she secured the scarves. "Because I can guarantee you're not going anywhere now."

He closed his eyes as her mouth started to roam his body.

He wasn't going anywhere.

Not yet, anyway.

5

LATER ON IN THE WEEK, Mari met with Lindsay at Lindsay's apartment, to talk about the restaurant's finances. She didn't want to talk about it at the restaurant, because she didn't want the crew to overhear and get nervous…and she didn't invite Lindsay to her place, because Nick was still curled up in her sheets, right where she'd left him. She hoped that the talk wouldn't take long. A quickie before the morning shift was just what her body wanted.

At least, it would hold her until that night.

Lindsay opened the door to her spacious apartment with a smile. Lindsay had made very good money as an accountant before she turned her efforts toward managing Mari's restaurant, and two restaurants her parents owned. Obviously her investments were holding up, Mari thought, letting out a low whistle. "Place looks great," she said, sitting down on one of Lindsay's Queen Anne couches.

"Thanks," Lindsay said absently, dropping down into a loveseat, oblivious to her surroundings. Instead, all her attention was focused on the paperwork strewn across her dark cherry wood coffee table. "The restaurant has been doing better…but we're not quite in the clear yet.''

''That's what I love about you, Lindsay,'' Mari said with a grin. ''You're an incurable optimist. Is that coffee I smell?''

''Help yourself. It's in the kitchen,'' Lindsay said. ''You're in an awfully good mood this morning. It's the review, isn't it?''

''Sort of,'' Mari hedged, smiling to herself in the kitchen. The review helped, sure…but last night's ''celebration'' of the review still had her in orbit.

She'd never let a man do to her all the things that Nick had done. She'd never felt about anyone the way she felt about Nick. She'd worry about the wisdom of that later.

He cared for her. And for the first time in longer than she could remember, she felt like it wasn't all on her shoulders.

She went back to Lindsay's living room, coffee in hand, grinning at the way her friend frowned over numbers. So serious, Mari thought.

She needed a ''celebration'' or two of her own. Mari giggled.

Lindsay looked up at her. ''What, have you been drinking this morning?''

''Nothing stronger than coffee,'' Mari replied. ''Let's get this over with.''

Lindsay still eyed her suspiciously, but then let it ride. ''All right. We're showing an upturn in finances, here,'' she pointed it out on the chart she'd built up.

"But we still need to hit this level to remain solvent and actually creep out of the red and into the black."

Mari listened, nodding as best she could. Unfortunately, two of the scarves they'd used last night were red and black, and that brought back memories...she had to suppress a sensual shudder.

"I still think entering a competition might not be a bad idea, but right now, we've got promotion going, so it might not matter...."

Mari nodded, still only half listening. She could only think of Nick, his strong hands...the way he'd pressed into her.

"And then we're going to have Santa do a strip tease on the roof."

Mari nodded absently. Nick, still curled up in her bed...

"Mari, are you even listening to me?"

Mari responded with a blink. "I'm sorry. What?"

"I've been making up the most awful promo stuff imaginable, and you just keep nodding like one of those bobble-head dolls." Lindsay's gaze bore into Mari's like an interrogation lamp. "All right. What gives?"

"Sorry," Mari said. "I've been a little distracted lately. I am glad we're doing better."

"But we're not in the clear yet," Lindsay warned again. "You're going to have to be on the ball with this, Mari."

Mari nodded again, solemnly. "All right. I will pay attention."

Lindsay sighed. "Maybe you'll want to work on some specials to get rid of the excess chicken, too."

Mari smiled at that. "Don't worry. We'll definitely be working on specials."

Now Lindsay leaned back and studied Mari, and for a moment, Mari felt the hint of a blush climb high on her cheeks, she looked away, but when she looked back, Lindsay was frowning. "What?" she asked.

"You're sleeping with him, aren't you?" Lindsay let out a slow breath. "You're actually sleeping with Nick."

Mari closed her eyes. "I know it's not a good idea...."

"He's your *employee*. Have you lost your mind?"

Mari shot a sharp glance at Lindsay. "Maybe I have."

"That's how you developed your new menu, isn't it?" Lindsay stood up and paced a little bit. "Mari, you didn't just let him come up with the menu because...well, because you two were..."

Mari glared at Lindsay now. "Come on, Lindsay. You know me better than that."

"I thought I did." Lindsay's voice was low. "What's going on with this?"

"I don't know." Mari hadn't really wanted to dwell on it. She'd wanted to enjoy the physical pleasure, maybe even indulge in the illusion of caring and comfort between them. But what was there, really? Was she just deluding herself?

Lindsay must have seen something on her face, because she sat down next to her. "Forget the restaurant for a minute," she said quietly, shifting gears from accountant to friend. "Mari, are you in love with him?"

Mari felt a little pang, deep in her chest. "I don't know," she responded. "It's been years since I've loved anybody...or thought I loved anybody. I really don't know."

And thinking about it scares the hell out of me.

"Mari," Lindsay said. "I feel like crap pointing this out, but...you don't think he's going to stay, do you?"

Mari looked at her, as if slapped. Lindsay's eyes were sorrowful.

"I've seen his resumé...and I've made some discreet inquiries," Lindsay said. "I mean, he's our sous-chef."

"You spied on him."

"I was thinking of you," Lindsay said, and to her credit, she *did* look like she felt badly about the whole thing. "He's ambitious. That's not even the right word. *Obsessive* might be the better word. He was a terror. He worked at Four Seasons before Phillip Marceau had him partner with him at Le Chapeau Noir. He placed third in the Internationale Culinary Competition, right here in the city, when he was with Blackstone's. He was primed to be the next Wolfgang Puck...hell. Maybe the next Escoffier or Bocuse. And then he was accused of stealing. I can see he'd do anything to get that back."

Mari thought about how caring he'd been last

night...the way he'd told her not to carry her worries all by herself. The way he'd let her lean on him.

"He cares about me, Lindsay."

"I don't doubt it," Lindsay said gently. "But I'm just trying to say...he cares about his career more, Mari. Don't forget that."

Mari felt her heart clutch painfully.

"I won't forget," Mari replied, the haze of euphoria from last night forgotten. "Let's go over those figures again. I want to see just how far out of the hole we are." She nodded resolutely. "Then *I'll* make plans from there."

THE FOLLOWING MONDAY, Nick waited at his house. Mari would be coming by later, after she finished going over the week's take and some financial plans with Lindsay. Lindsay, he noticed, had been distinctly cold to him the past week, the few times he'd run into her. Either Mari had told her what they'd been up to besides menu planning, or Lindsay had put it together for herself, but either way the message was clear...Lindsay didn't want him messing around with her best friend and business partner.

He shrugged it off. It wasn't pleasant, granted—but then, it wasn't her business, either. What he did with Mari when they weren't in the restaurant was just between him and her.

He smiled. And he was looking forward to it.

He glanced at his watch and forced himself to stay focused. Since Mari wasn't going to be coming until later, he felt safe in inviting another guest here in the meantime. This visitor was the reason he was nervous.

There was a knock on his door, and he tried not to spring to answer it. "Hi, David," Nick said, his voice calm and friendly. "I'm really glad you could stop by."

David Armand stepped in, a tall, thin man in his thirties, and one of the top writers for *Saveur* magazine. He'd called Nick up out of the blue, after several of the newspaper articles on Guilty Pleasures had hit—David had done several positive pieces on Nick in the past, once when he was with Blackstone's, once with Le Chapeau Noir. He wanted to do an article on Nick's new job. Nick was hoping he'd help with getting the word out now...not only was Nick *not* embezzling or being brought up on any sort of charges, he was turning around a small restaurant.

Nick felt sure Mari would understand. It would be good publicity for the restaurant.

Of course, you haven't told her about the article, either.

"Can I offer you anything? Thirsty? Something to eat?" Nick said instead.

David shook his head. "No, I'm fine. I just wanted to get into the article, if that's okay with you."

"That's fine with me," Nick said, sitting in an armchair across from David's seat on the couch.

David brought out a tape recorder and a spiral notepad, going through the motions of recording Nick's acceptance of taping the session. Then the questions started.

''So…Nick Avery, former chef at Blackstone's and Le Chapeau Noir, now at a restaurant with the unlikely name of Guilty Pleasures.''

Nick grinned. ''It seems strange, yes…''

''What happened?''

Nick felt his guard go up by inches. David's face was impassive, but the question…Nick shrugged it off. David had always been kind and complimentary in his writing. That was why Nick agreed to this. *Maybe it's just my defensiveness,* Nick told himself. ''I enjoy working at Guilty Pleasures. It's fun, and it's also a challenge. We've come up with a really outrageous menu, and we offer a complete experience…you don't just go for the food, you go for the atmosphere, the whole nine yards.''

David jotted down a few careless notes, but his eyes seemed fixed on Nick. ''So, the bad location is just one more challenge?''

Nick suppressed a wince. ''I prefer to think of it as undiscovered,'' he said smoothly. ''Besides, people who love food don't mind the unpretentiousness of the neighborhood.''

David snorted. ''Well, that's one way of putting it. And the whole sexy-menu thing?''

Nick nodded, on more solid ground now. ''Food should be a sensual celebration. So should sex. What better comparison than a fabulous meal and a seduction, right?''

He thought of Mari, the taste of her, and smiled.

David seemed to note the smile. ''Well. So you

don't miss doing the classical French menu, or something more traditional?''

Nick thought about it. ''I've had more fun and more opportunity to be creative with this menu than I have with any other menu in years,'' he said, and realized as he said it how true it was. It had started out as a lark, then a bold move made out of desperation. It was now something he was genuinely enjoying.

''So. Why did you get fired from Le Chapeau Noir?''

Nick blinked at David. ''I'm sorry?''

''The whole restaurant community knows that you got fired from Chapeau in a cloud of scandal,'' David said, his tone never changing. ''What is your response to that?''

Nick stared for a second, feeling an icy fist clench in his stomach.

''That's what this is all about, isn't it?'' Nick said in a low voice. ''You don't care about Guilty Pleasures. You want to find out what the hell happened at Chapeau.''

To his credit, David finally looked a little uncomfortable. ''That's where the real story is, Nick,'' he said, as if pleading. ''I've been doing puff pieces on famous chefs for years. They're making budget cuts at the magazine. If I don't come up with something really breaking, they're going to cut *me*.''

''And that's my problem?'' Nick said coldly. ''You want me to come up with dirt for you to publish?''

''Everybody wants to know what happened,'' David said persuasively. ''Phillip Marceau isn't talking, but that's because his lawyers and that bulldog father of his won't let him. You, on the other hand…nobody's approached you because you disappeared. Next thing I see, you're in some hole-in-the-wall in the Mission District, with a raunchy menu and a no-star rating. What happened to drive the mighty Nick Avery to this? *That's* a story!''

Nick stood up, clicking off the tape recorder. ''I think this interview is over.''

''But you could tell *your* side of the story,'' David continued. ''Don't you want that? Nobody's ever gone up against the Marceaus. That could be a hell of a coup!''

Nick thought about it. ''Sure, I could bad-mouth Phillip…but then those lawyers you've mentioned would be after *me,* right? And besides, I've put it behind me.'' That was a lie, he realized, but he moved doggedly onward. ''The most important thing in my life right now is Guilty Pleasures, and the work I'm doing there.''

''You've got to be kidding me,'' David groaned, picking up the recorder and shoving it in his pocket. ''Come on. I remember the last interview I did with you. You were ready to light the world on fire with a blowtorch. Now I'm supposed to believe that Nick Avery's gone *soft?*''

Nick could picture himself planting a punch right on the tall man's jaw. *Gone soft, my ass, pal.* But what would that accomplish? He'd get put in jail, and David would *really* have a story to write about. Nick just walked to the door, opening it. ''Just get out.''

Before David could make it, Mari walked in. "Why, thank you," she said, leaning up and kissing him quickly, her violet eyes ablaze. Then she saw he had company, and blushed a little. "I'm sorry. I'm early."

"That's okay," Nick said. "David was just leaving."

"You must be Mari…Mari Salazar," David said swiftly, and Nick glared at him. "I read about you in the *Guardian*.…"

Abruptly, David trailed off as he studied Mari's face.

"Wait a minute," David said. "I know you."

Mari, Nick noticed, went pale.

"You're Marion Worthington!" David snapped his fingers. "You were the one from Le Pome!"

Mari's back went ramrod-straight. "I think Nick said you were just leaving?"

"And now you're in business with Nick," David mused. "Man. The failure of Le Pome was downright legendary. Is that what made you change your name? How did you wind up working with Nick, anyway? Maybe I could interview you.…"

Nick moved on David, his arms clenching with menace. He gave him a shove toward the door. "You heard her. Get out."

David grimaced. "You can't stop me from writing this story."

"*Out.*" With one last push, Nick shut the door behind David.

"So. This was what you had to do this afternoon?"

Her tone was conversational, but he could see the wounded look in her eyes. "I wouldn't have interrupted, but Lindsay and I got done early."

"It was a mistake," Nick said, feeling a wave of guilt. "I thought he was going to do a promotional piece on Guilty Pleasures. I've worked with him before.... He didn't used to be like this."

"So. You wanted to do a promotional piece on my restaurant," Mari mused, "but you didn't want to tell me beforehand or have me be involved."

She let the words hang in the air. Then she headed for the door herself. Nick stepped in front of her.

"It was a mistake," he said sharply. "I made a mistake, okay?"

"Now he knows," she hissed instead. "He knows who I am. I thought I'd buried that whole mess, and now it's getting kicked up again because *you* wanted to get some publicity, for the fine job *you* were doing with *my* restaurant!"

She pushed past him, and Nick held her against him before she could open the door. "You're right," he said, and she snarled at him. "I was trying to get publicity. I was trying to get my reputation back on track. I'm sorry if it hurt you. I didn't mean for it to hurt you."

She spun to look at him. "And what about all that stuff...'Don't worry, Mari. Lean on me, Mari. Let me take care of things.'" She glared at him. "This is how you *take care of things,* huh?"

"Mari..."

"No. Don't talk to me, Nick," she said, tugging away. "I don't want to see you right now."

With that, she walked out, slamming the door behind her.

THAT NIGHT, MARI SAT on her couch, staring at her TV but not really seeing it. She didn't call Lindsay because, although Lindsay was too good a friend to say "I told you so," Mari would still sense it...and she felt stupid enough right now.

You don't honestly think he'll stay, do you?

That was the problem, Mari thought, shutting off the TV and pacing around her living room. After their last night together, when he'd gotten her to relinquish control and consequently showed her that he wanted to help her, she'd trusted him...and some traitorous part of her heart had thought, for just a moment, that he *wouldn't* leave. Lindsay's words had brought reality in to a certain extent, but her heart apparently hadn't been convinced.

At least, she thought with a pang, not until this afternoon.

He went to a reporter. Behind my back.

Nick was a scheming opportunist, Mari thought, hitting a pillow. He was a conniving, seducing rat. He was...

She closed her eyes against tears. *Why can't he care about me?*

She was now hitting the pillows so hard that she didn't hear the door knock. She wondered how long it had been going on. She peered out her peephole.

Nick stared back at her.

She thought for a moment of just leaving him out in the hallway. Still, she was in a fighting mood...and here was the object of her ire, conveniently showing up.

She yanked open the door. "You're a jerk," she said, without preamble, but to her disgrace, her voice trembled.

His eyes looked sorrowful, and he made no rebuttal to her accusation. "Mind if I come in?" he said instead.

Her eyes widened. "For what? Because I think your days of *taking care of me* are over," she spat out.

"I'm not here to sleep with you," he said, his voice tired. "I'm here to apologize."

That took some of the wind out of her sails. She still looked at him with suspicion, but she did let him come in. *Let him try to apologize,* her subconscious thought. *Then kick his sorry ass out.*

Still, that small, stupid part of her heart began to hope.

He was wearing a pair of Dockers and a button-up shirt, a little less casual than his usual jeans and T-shirt. He sat down on her couch.

"I don't know that you'll want to sit down," she said, leaning against her desk. "I don't think you're going to be here that long."

The words were bitchy, she knew that. At this point, she didn't care.

"I didn't want to hurt you, but you're right.... I was thinking more of myself."

Her eyebrows went up. "A novel way to start an apology."

"I never pretended…" he started, then let out a gruff breath, rubbing his hands over his face as if he could wipe the weariness off with his fingers. "No. That's a cop-out. I got a job with you because it was the only job I could get at the time. I worked with you on the menu because I saw it as a way out—and because I could be alone with you."

She swallowed, hard. What he'd described, except for the job, was what she had felt…what she had convinced herself that she'd felt.

So why are you blaming him for doing what you thought you were doing?

Because it had moved past that, she thought. At least, for her it had moved past that. That thought worried her more than any of the previous ones.

"What do you know about me, Mari?"

She sat down at the far side of the couch, sinking into the cushions. "Not a lot," she said, shrugging. "I know where you've worked. I know that you competed when you were with Blackstone's, you worked at the Four Seasons, and of course I know about Le Chapeau Noir…."

"Did you know about me when you went to the Culinary School?"

She had her first smile of the night at that. "I barely knew my own name when I went to the Culinary," she said ruefully, remembering the ragged pace, the constant work…the competitive spirit as well as the friendship. "No, I hadn't heard of you."

"I got kicked out," he said, with a small half grin. "Leon managed to get me back in, but it was a near thing."

Her eyes widened. This was definitely not what she expected to hear tonight—but she was fascinated, nonetheless.

"It was my second year," Nick mused, and she could see from his far-off gaze that he wasn't in the living room with her at that moment—he was back in Upstate New York, probably in his early twenties, with no reputation to lose or gain back. "I'd gotten in on a scholarship. I'm originally from Covina, down in Southern Cal. Not a great neighborhood...in fact, our house was right on the border of the *barrio*. My mother worked in restaurants to keep me in private school. I'm not saying that for pity...I'm just saying, she worked really hard, and I worked in restaurants too...summers, after school. I knew that cooking was what I wanted to do, and when I got the scholarship to the Culinary, she was so proud of me, she got me a set of knives."

He sounded almost embarrassed, saying it, but Mari was touched. Most parents wouldn't have under-stood...hers certainly hadn't. When she'd said she was going to the Culinary, they'd been unpleasantly sur-prised. Chefs didn't make money, not unless they were famous.

Which is why they worked on making you famous as soon as you graduated. An effort that had ulti-mately failed. She focused on Nick's story, trying to keep her errant thoughts together.

Cathy Yardley 127

"Anyway, I was doing pretty well…and I got along with Leon. I guess it got a couple of the upperclassmen steamed. Especially when I got the internship to Blackstone's when they didn't." His smile was feral now, and she could see the competition gleaming in his eyes. "So my knives got stolen. People had lost knives before…not a whole set, but it happened. But most people could afford to replace their knives, too. I couldn't afford another job, and my scholarship wouldn't cover it. When I found who'd stolen them, he said it was a prank." He ran his finger through his hair. "I wasn't amused."

"What'd you do?" Mari asked, feeling a chill of foreboding.

"Well, I wasn't going to do anything…just grab my stuff and leave. Maybe report him, if Leon insisted I should. He was getting close to being my mentor at the time." He took a deep breath. "But the guy started talking trash. He said I'd never amount to anything…that I'd be flipping burgers at a truck-stop with my crappy set of knives. Said that I was just ghetto anyway, and that they'd just given me the scholarship and the internship to get some publicity, like 'poor kid makes good' or something. So I wound up pounding him. Pretty badly, actually."

"So they kicked you out," Mari summarized.

"Turns out the kid was from the governor's family," Nick said, with a small, bitter laugh. "Thankfully, the governor wasn't too fond of the kid, either— guess he was just a whiny little jerk that was about to flunk out of school anyway. At least, that's the angle Leon played when he got me back in.''

''I'm sorry,'' Mari said, and meant it. She didn't want to, but she slid slightly closer to him on the couch. ''But Nick…what does this have to do with us? With this afternoon?''

He sighed. ''I guess I'm just trying to show you that I worked too hard to get to where I was at Le Chapeau Noir. I didn't get a damned *parking ticket* after that scrape at the Culinary. I didn't have a steady girlfriend, and the only friend I had—such as he was—was a kid named Phillip Marceau, who was so driven he made me look laid back.''

Mari's breath hitched. ''Phillip, the guy…'' She started to say *who fired you?* but changed it to the more diplomatic. ''From Le Chapeau Noir?''

Nick nodded, and his eyes burned. ''The same. The bottom line, which I can't seem to get to, is that nothing in my life has been more important than succeeding. I almost had it when I was at Chapeau. A few more years, and I would have had the money to open a second restaurant, and that would have been *all* mine…my menu, my choices, my name over the door.''

She heard the vehemence in his voice. *This really is a bad apology,* she thought inanely. *He's trying to explain that…*

He looked at her, and for the first time since he'd walked in, the bitterness wasn't in his eyes. Instead, it was warmth and passion…and confusion.

PLAY THE Lucky Key Game

Do You Have the LUCKY KEY?

and you can get

FREE BOOKS
and a FREE GIFT!

Scratch the gold areas with a coin. Then check below to see the books and gift you can get!

▶ DETACH AND POST CARD TODAY! ▶

YES!
I have scratched off the gold areas. Please send me the **2 FREE BOOKS** and **GIFT** for which I qualify. I understand I am under no obligation to purchase any books, as explained on the back of this card. I am over 18 years of age.

K4BI

Mrs/Miss/Ms/Mr   Initials

BLOCK CAPITALS PLEASE

Surname

Address

Postcode

🔑🔑🔑🔑 2 free books plus a free gift   🔑🔑🔑🔑 1 free book

🔑🔑🔑🔑 2 free books   🔑🔑🔑🔑 Try Again!

Visit us online at
www.millsandboon.co.uk

The Reader Service™ — Here's how it works:

Accepting the free books places you under no obligation to buy anything. You may keep the books and gift and return the despatch note marked 'cancel'. If we do not hear from you, about a month later we'll send you 4 brand new books (2 Blaze Romance™ and 2 Sensual Romance™) and invoice you just £11.18* each. That's the complete price - there is no extra charge for postage and packing. You may cancel at any time, otherwise every month we'll send you 4 more books, which you may either purchase or return to us - the choice is yours.

*Terms and prices subject to change without notice.

NO STAMP NEEDED!

THE READER SERVICE™
FREE BOOK OFFER
FREEPOST CN81
CROYDON
CR9 3WZ

If offer card is missing write to: The Reader Service, PO Box 236, Croydon, CR9 3RU

NO STAMP
NECESSARY
IF POSTED IN
THE U.K. OR N.I.

She knew the look. Hell, she wore the look often when it came to Nick.

"The other night..." he said, and his voice went uneven "...I didn't think about the fact that we might be getting crappy reviews or that you might fire me or that you wouldn't let me get my ideas on the menu. I wasn't thinking about how to get my name out and get successful. I was only thinking about *you*. About helping you out and making you feel better." He let out a deep breath. "And it scared the hell out of me."

She blinked.

"I guess I agreed to the reporter to reassure myself that I wasn't getting sidetracked," he said. "I didn't mean to hurt you, and I really am sorry."

Mari processed that for a minute.

"I don't want to hurt you," he said again, and his fingers stroked the side of her face...a featherlight touch. "I won't do something like that again."

"Don't say something you don't mean," she whispered back.

He leaned forward and kissed her. It was gentle, undemanding.

"I promise," he said. "I won't hurt you again."

She let him kiss her again, the heat of the promise turning into a heat of an entirely different sort. She leaned into it, noticing that there was some saltiness to the kiss.

That's when she realized...a few tears had inched their way down her cheeks. She rubbed them away hastily.

"You'd better not," she said, and kissed him back, hard.

6

THE KITCHEN WAS A NOISY, chaotic swell of activity, and Nick was manning the helm. He couldn't believe it was almost three months that he'd been there, and that the new menu had been selling at a brisk rate for two months.

After several hours of the lunch shift and heading into dinner, he felt like he'd been working here for years. And at the gratifyingly smooth workings of the crew as they shifted into high gear, he felt like he'd been working with *them* for years.

"We are *so* packed, it's nuts," Zooey said, in her high, girlish voice. "Where's Mari, again?"

Paulo was busy working the sauté station, his hands a blur of motion as he spiced one saucier pan here, and plated an entrée there. Tiny was working the grill, making the flames leap like he was some kind of demon-chef. Nick noticed that they were too busy to answer.

"Mari's off at the landlord's," Nick said, barely looking up from his own work, although he was startled into glancing up at the boo that resounded among the crew.

"That chiseling old bastard," Tiny pronounced, the flames punctuating his response.

"Yeah. Slumlord," Paulo said with a snort. "Ten bucks says he ups the rent because he heard we were doing well!"

There was a rowdy chorus of assent on that one. "Don't worry, Mari can handle him," Nick responded, and there was more assent at that…and they were a little calmer, too. Nick didn't know the landlord, but he knew Mari, and he doubted any chiseling old bastard landlord could get the drop on her.

Few people could, he thought, with a proud smile. She was a sharp, savvy, no-holds-barred woman.

She was incredible.

He'd spent as many nights as he could at her place, or had encouraged her to stay with him, especially on Sundays, so they could spend a leisurely Monday morning over the paper, or wandering through the market. They'd spent a lot of it in bed, but they'd spent more time out of it, he'd noticed…not just having sex, but having dinner, talking over plans for the restaurant. Or just talking.

Their relationship was moving into affair country, he noticed. He still wasn't sure how he felt about that, but another part of him realized it was going to continue to happen, no matter what he logically thought.

He cared about her too much.

Tonight, they were going to work on some modifications to the menu…and maybe broach the idea of entering in one of the competitions. Nothing as prestigious as Internationale or the Bocuse D'or in France, he amended. Guilty Pleasures was still too new in the game, and still had a lot of seasoning before it was ready to handle the big-league competitors that those venues drew. But some smaller, more local stuff would be good confidence builders, he thought. And he knew Lindsay had been talking about doing some more promo stuff. He told Mari he'd go over some of her plans with her, just sort of brainstorm.

He'd also promised her to make more of the chocolate dessert he'd made the first night he'd spent over there, he thought with a smile. All work and no play made Nick a dull boy, had been her statement. The sensual promise in her eyes had been more than enough encouragement.

"Hey, *jefe*," Paulo said, nudging him. "You still awake? Ready on seven?"

Nick jerked his head. "Huh? Oh. Sorry."

Tiny laughed. "I know that look. Thinking about a woman, huh?"

The whole crew laughed at this one, and Nick was surprised to hear them gibing with him…joking with him.

"She pretty?" Paulo said, as he and Nick put the orders in the window. "Maybe you could give her my number!"

"She's too much woman for you," Nick said, his own tone light.

"Yeah?" Tiny said. "For Paulo, that ain't hard."

"Shut up, *ese*." Paulo made a mock growl at the huge grill man. "I make plenty women happy."

"Yeah. When you walk away, dwarf-boy."

The crew continued in this vein, and Nick smiled. They were really working hard, but their camaraderie hadn't faded into enmity like he'd seen happen when Blackstone's went into overdrive. In fact, they were holding up better than some seasoned crews he'd seen.

Zooey smiled at him, showing him a dessert she'd made. "I tried it out during my break," she said, the youth in her smile showing her nervousness. "Think you could try it?"

He nodded. "Sure. What do you call it?"

She blushed. "Lemongasm," she said, then frowned as Paulo hooted. "What? It goes with the menu!"

"I'd be happy to try it," Nick said, ignoring the rest of the crews yelps of *Hey, so would I!*, and the like. Her answering grin was enough.

He was surprised to find himself whistling as he plated up three more orders in quick succession. Mari wasn't the only one he was proud of, he realized. It'd be hard to find a better crew—nor a more loyal one. He'd miss them when he left.

He frowned as he pushed plates into the window.

If I leave.

"Nick?"

Nick turned. It was Mo, not manning his usual position at the host's podium. "Problem?" Nick said immediately.

"Nope. Just somebody who wanted to compliment the chefs," Mo said proudly, adding in a whisper, "the guy has a *way* expensive suit on. Okay to bring him back?"

Nick felt his back straighten. It wasn't often, but he remembered getting requests like this back at Chapeau…usually after one or another article about the restaurant and his work there was printed up. It would be fun, he decided. Hell, the crew could use the morale boost. "Sure," Nick said, straightening his black shirt and glancing at the crew. Most of their more colorful slogans were covered with aprons anyway. "Go ahead and send him back."

The crew, he noticed, were also standing straighter…and several of them were grinning. Nick was grinning, too, until the man stepped into the kitchen. Then, abruptly, all of his emotion drained in an icy wash.

"Phillip Marceau," Nick said, his voice toneless. "Glad to see you're enjoying my work."

Phillip didn't look a bit different. Hair a shade too pale for his tanned skin, blue eyes sharp as ever, and an air of superiority that only years of the finest schools and expensive locales could instill. His dove gray suit was expensive—Nick had bought one like it himself in charcoal, back in his first days as a well-paid head chef. Phillip looked around the kitchen with an air of supercilious disdain. "I was so charmed by the menu, I wanted to compliment you in person, Nick."

Nick hadn't realized his hands had bunched into fists until they tightened with menace. "Must be a nice change from the tired *foie gras* you're plating up over at Chapeau," Nick replied.

"Especially the…what was it? Oh, yes. The

Mélange-à-trois.'' Phillip's voice held a hint of cruel laughter. "I've half a mind to contact *Bon Appetit* and tell them to get the recipe.''

"Why? So you can change the name and add it to Chapeau's menu?" Nick replied pleasantly. "If you need new ideas so badly, I could probably pencil it down for you.''

Phillip's face soured. Nick knew that Phillip was an excellent manager, but creativity had never been his strong suit, and they both knew it.

"You haven't changed, I see. Still making juvenile jokes.''

Nick grinned. "I see you still haven't developed a sense of humor.''

Phillip's smile was sharp. "Au contraire. I find the world infinitely more amusing since you've moved on from my restaurant. Especially now that you're *here*…and producing such, ah, *quality* work.''

Should'a done something about you when you fired me. Nick smiled at Phillip, picturing that angelic face sporting a black eye and a fat lip.

"Hey, Nick," Paulo said, his arms crossed, with Tiny standing threateningly behind him. "Who's the *pendejo?*''

Nick grinned at the insult, knowing that Phillip always relied on translators and really didn't know much Spanish, much less swearing in Spanish. "Nobody important," Nick answered. "Just somebody who likes to think he's a chef.''

He saw that both the original insult and the casual

response had the desired effect. Phillip's thin lips drew into a tight line.

"Well, after August, I guess I won't be the only one who thinks I'm a chef," he replied, his tone oily and lethal. "Le Chapeau Noir is going to be entered in the Internationale Culinary Competition. It's over in Union Square this year, did you know?" His smile suggested that Nick didn't…that he was so far out of the culinary world, he didn't even know the location of one of their largest events. "So while you're serving up penis-shaped pasta here in the slums, spare me a thought, won't you?"

"Hey, Fifth Avenue." Tiny's voice was low, and his upper arms flexed with menace. "I don't care who you are. Take a walk, or take a beating."

"You don't *know* who I am," Phillip said with a sneer…but Nick noticed him take a step back, nonetheless. "And apparently, you don't even know who *he* is."

"Sure we do," Zooey piped in, to Nick's surprise. "He's Nick!"

"He's our sous-chef," Paulo added. "The best."

Before Nick could feel warmed by their show of support, Phillip went and ruined it. "Sous-chef?" His voice was gleeful. "Can't even manage head chef anymore, huh, Nick? Even in a dump like this."

"The head chef's the owner," Nick said. "Not that I owe you an explanation."

"Ah. The owner. Mari Salazar…or should I say, Marion Worthington?" Phillip must have noticed Nick's shock, because his smile was evil-looking.

"Thought I wouldn't know, hmm? I was having a long talk with David from *Saveur* yesterday…. He's writing up Le Chapeau Noir. He just happened to have a few choice things to say about your new boss, Nick. Especially about her spectacular failures. You two must be a match made in heaven."

"Right." Nick felt a safety valve inside him snap. "Now you're going to get yours."

Phillip's eyes widened, and he took another step toward the door. "You wouldn't dare," he said, but his voice wasn't so sure of it.

"But *I* would," Tiny said, cracking his knuckles. "Nobody talks shit about Mari."

The rest of the crew advanced on Phillip, right down to Zooey, who was brandishing a marble rolling pin like she meant business.

"Fine." Phillip shot one last glare at Nick. "I see you've finally found your niche, Nick. You never were cut out for a four-star, anyway. Enjoy working as a sous-chef next door to an adult theater then. You're never going to earn the money or the rep to open your own restaurant. And you're never going to be in my league."

"I never *was* in your league, Phillip," Nick said. "I was *better.*"

With that, Phillip turned and left, a scowl on his face.

"Who was that guy?" Zooey said, peering out the window at Phillip's retreating form.

"Whatever you did, he probably deserved it," Paulo observed with a shrug.

"Watch the grill," Tiny said with a growl, handing a metal spatula to Xavier. "I'm still going to kick that guy's—"

"Easy," Nick said, putting a hand up. "He's not worth it. He's rich and he's got a team of blood-sucking lawyers, and he's vindictive as hell." Nick paused. "That's why I haven't gone after him. You don't want to be cooking in jail."

Tiny shrugged. "Like it'd be the first time." Still, he turned back to his grill.

Nick took a deep breath. "Okay, orders are up, we're still busy. We've still got a few hours left before the next shift comes on. Don't worry about that jerk. Let's just focus."

Thankfully, the crew did as instructed, although he felt a grim mood replace the earlier joking.

Nick tried to follow his own advice, but he kept getting sidetracked by Phillip's one, poisonous comment.

Enjoy working as a sous-chef next door to an adult theater then. You're never going to earn the money or the rep to open your own restaurant. And you're never going to be in my league.

Nick growled as he plated up a few pear-and-gorgonzola salads and tried Zooey's new dessert. He had been happy, thinking of Mari, thinking of how much she was beginning to mean to him. Now, he had this to think about.

It would hurt less, Nick thought, if Phillip hadn't been so close to being right. Guilty Pleasures was a great place, and Mari beyond a great woman. But if he stayed, he wouldn't be a four-star chef. He wouldn't make enough money, and the only way he could accomplish his old dream would be to leave.

I promise I won't hurt you again.

He closed his eyes for a second, then opened them. "Ready on five," he said.

He wouldn't hurt her. He meant that.

He just wondered how badly he'd be hurting himself if he stayed.

MARI WAITED NERVOUSLY in the lobby of her landlord's rental property office, which was a run-down old stucco building that always looked in need of repair. *Not a promising sight for people looking to rent,* Mari thought, clutching her purse. *But then, beggars can't be choosers.*

Her landlord, Jack MacDonald, preferred beggars for tenants. And Mari had been one when she'd come looking for a cheap property for Guilty Pleasures.

Jack came out of the closed door of his office, smiling like a used-car salesman as he showed out a young couple who looked happy. Mari got the feeling that Jack had promised them the moon, and they'd signed something.

Still, she thought as she stood up, they looked young and in love. Whatever they got probably *would* seem like a palace, from that viewpoint. It might not be much, but it would be *theirs*.

Mari felt a momentary pang, and she wasn't sure if it was sadness at their naiveté…or envy for their happiness.

"Mari! Come on in." Jack ushered her into his cheaply decorated office, with its peeling desktop and ugly taupe file cabinets. "So…lease is coming up."

"If we're going to be talking lease renegotiation, I have to insist that my business partner Lindsay be here," Mari said, in her most businesslike voice. "Unless you're willing to have another year on the same terms. Anything longer or any change in the rent, and we'll definitely need to reschedule, so Lindsay can be involved."

"No, no, nothing that formal," Jack said, his laugh friendly. Mari's guard immediately went up. "I'm just notifying tenants in that block of some new information."

Mari went still. "What new information?"

"That you're not going to be renting from me anymore." Jack's smile was wide enough to split his face in half. "I finally got somebody to buy those buildings."

Mari's stomach clenched into a frozen ball. *New owner.* That could mean anything. Rent increased at a huge rate. Everybody evicted. Or the buildings torn down…

Stay calm, Mari said. "Oh? Who is this new owner?"

"It's part of a conglomerate," Jack said, waving his hand. "Something about renovating the neighborhood, and I think it's great that somebody's doing it."

"Somebody other than you, you mean," Mari muttered.

"Huh?"

"Nothing. So when does the new owner take over?"

"Two months," Jack said. He was downright ebullient. This conglomerate must be coughing up some hefty cash to make the man this chipper. "I'm sure he'll want to keep you on. I hear you're making some really nice money these days...and if the place gets renovated, you'll probably get even more business."

And get charged even higher rent. Mari stood up. "I'll pass this on to Lindsay."

"I'll send out something official-looking," Jack said, standing up also. "I'm sure Lindsay will want something on paper and all."

"I'm sure she will," Mari echoed.

"Don't be a stranger, now!" Jack said, waving Mari out of the office.

Mari walked back to her car, numb. Lindsay had warned her about the possibility of her rent being raised, but there were legal limits to how much a landlord could raise in a year. Besides, business *had* been better...she felt like she had some breathing room.

Who would have thought her place would get bought out?

She got in her car, started the engine. Now, she was facing possible eviction...or at the very least, a lot steeper rent. Which was almost the same thing, considering the huge rents anywhere else in San Francisco. She certainly couldn't afford to *buy* her own space.

Do not panic, she told herself sternly as she zipped her way back to her loft. *Things will turn around.*

Look at what happened just a few months ago, after all. She'd hired Nick, which had been a gamble…she'd tried a new menu, which was a big risk, especially with its chancy theme and questionable-sounding content. Now, she was finally creeping in the black and happier than she'd been since she opened.

So why not take another risk?

She found a parking spot on the street—a good omen, she thought, considering the near-impossible parking conditions in the city—and went back to her apartment to change into her work clothes. The thought of taking a risk would not leave her mind.

She called up Lindsay, leaving a message that they'd need to talk, not wanting to break the potentially bad news to her over the phone. As she hung up, her gaze caught on one of the flyers Lindsay had left in a bundle of paperwork on Mari's desk.

Internationale Culinary Competition. Grand prize: one hundred and fifty thousand dollars.

That wasn't much, relatively speaking, Mari thought. She'd sunk half a million in Guilty Pleasures. But it would be a cushion until they found a new place…or maybe a down payment for a new place. And the promotional benefits would be enormous.

And maybe, just maybe, there would be a financier who was interested in their unusual style…interested enough to invest.

So why not? The entry fee was a little steep, but as her father used to say, you have to spend money to make money. It was one of the few bits of advice that had stuck with her.

Are you crazy? Her subconscious nagged at her. The people who entered Internationale were all four-star types...internationally known. They were stars of the culinary scene. The competition was about two months away. They'd probably be preparing for this for a year, at least. And they would have top-ranked chefs working on it.

Nick's a top-ranked chef. And before Le Pome, I wasn't a slouch, either. Before her confidence had been so badly shaken, she had been convinced that she could have entered the lofty echelon of top-ranked chefs. Then she'd convinced herself she didn't need the approval of the culinary world.

She still didn't need their approval, she thought. But she'd take their money...and make her name doing it. She knew her crew, and she knew Nick. She'd been around restaurants all her life, had been working in them since she graduated from the Culinary.

They were good enough. Good enough to take the added pressure of a short deadline, and *run* with it.

Good enough to win, if they only tried....

She picked up the phone, suppressing the jumble of nerves that pulled at her in favor of the excitement that was rushing through her veins. ''Hello? Yes. Is this the main office for the Internationale competition?'' she asked. ''Is it too late to enter? Could you fax me an entry form?''

BY THE END OF THE evening shift, Nick was exhausted. He'd been there for hours. There hadn't been any major hitches, granted, but he had to admit…Phillip's conversation had really thrown him for a loop.

He felt the dull throb of a headache, just behind his temples. Closing wasn't too far off now. He was surprised he hadn't seen Mari yet, though. He was looking forward to seeing her later…and spending some time with her. At this point, he didn't even need the oblivion of sex. He would be more than happy with just breathing in her floral-spicy scent and feeling her arms around him.

Well, the sex would be nice, too, he thought with a small grin. But that could wait for later.

Mari bounced in, and the first thing he noticed was her energy. She seemed to be suffused with it, moving with frenetic little bursts. She was smiling widely.

"So. I guess things with the landlord went well?" he said, basking in the warmth of her smile.

"Huh? Oh. No. Actually they went really…" She glanced around, seeing the crew staring at her. He could tell that she edited her response. "You guys know how Jack is."

Again, a rumble of commentary, just like the morning shift. This landlord must be some kind of jerk to be this widely known, Nick thought. He wondered what had occurred, but realized Mari would probably tell him later, when they were alone. Still, it couldn't have been that bad—she was practically dancing with happiness.

"But I got an idea," she said, "and I really think we can do a lot with it."

"Really?" Her enthusiasm was infectious. "So. What's your idea?"

"I'm entering us in a competition!"

"A competition?" Tiny asked. Tiny was working a double shift, as was Zooey—*we're really going to need to think of bringing on some more employees,* Nick thought. Then grinned, as he realized he was thinking like one of the owners. "What's the big deal about that?"

"Competitions are good," Nick replied. "They help get your name out, they give you a chance to show your stuff. Good publicity. Some of them have cash prizes."

"Whoo-hoo!" Tiny yelled, and the rest of the crew laughed.

"Yeah, I figure…those high-brow society kitchens haven't seen a fight till they compete with our crew," Mari said. He knew she was right. They were scrappers, every one of them—unorthodox, but definitely gifted, both with persistence and a keen sense of teamwork. They'd probably do very well, especially in one of the smaller competitions…something local, or out in one of the smaller towns. There probably wouldn't be a cash prize involved, but they were just starting out.

"When is it?" Antonio, their night runner, asked.

"Not for two months," Mari said.

"Two months?" Zooey wailed. "That's not a lot of time to prep!"

Nick interrupted again. "It's not so bad. It's sort of like Iron Chef…you know, you get an ingredient—or they say 'you have to have a fish meal, a meat meal, and a dessert' or something. You have all your stuff there at the beginning of the competition, you've got a set number of hours. Then there's judging, and you're all set."

"Doesn't sound that bad," Tiny said, nudging Zooey. "*We* could do that, easy."

"Competitions can be fun," Nick said, remembering his own experiences in competition…back in the day, as Tiny would say. "I think you guys could be pretty good at them."

"Regardless, this one will be worth it," Mari said, and her eyes shone. "And we're going to bust our butts until competition day, to win. Right?"

"Right!" The crew yelled as one, and Nick smiled again. They were now chattering excitedly to themselves.

"Orders are up, people," Nick said, wishing he could kiss Mari's full, smiling mouth. He felt better than he had in hours. They grumbled good-naturedly and went back to work, and he tugged Mari into the back room, doing what he'd wanted to before… pressing a kiss against her pliant lips. She parted them willingly, kissing him with enough force to make him hard. He pulled away, his breathing harsh.

"Well. I guess you had a good afternoon," he said, allowing himself one squeeze before stepping away from her and trying to force his body back to some semblance of calm. "So. What competition are we entering, anyway? Gilroy? Something in the East Bay?''

''No,'' she said, and hugged him. ''We're going to enter in Internationale!''

Her words stunned him. *''What?''*

She blinked. ''Internationale. You know the competition... I understand you were on Blackstone's team, the year they ranked fourth.''

''You can't be serious.''

That took some of the spring out of her step, and he saw her surprise. ''Well, why not?''

''Do you know the kind of teams that enter Internationale?'' Nick said, still shocked by her revelation. ''Henri's, Four Seasons, all the best restaurants in the country compete! And you're going to enter....''

Her eyes glinted, a dangerous violet blue. ''Guilty Pleasures. Yes, I am. I know it's not a lot of time....''

''It's more than not a lot of time,'' Nick said, lowering his voice. ''It's a suicidal deadline. I mean, we'd have to pick a team of six, we'd have to come up with a theme, a menu, we'd have to practice putting it together....''

''I know,'' Mari said, and there was a stubborn set to her lips. ''But look how quickly we got the menu together...and how well it worked out.''

Nick closed his eyes. The woman was serious...and she was determined. This was going to be very, very bad.

''That was different,'' he said. ''We still had time to tweak it. We had a full month to just set things up…and they weren't that difficult. Nothing that the crew couldn't handle.''

"The crew is up for more than you give them credit for," Mari said, and there was an edge of stiffness in her voice. "You'd be surprised."

"I'd have to be more than surprised for them to hold up to Internationale standards," Nick said. "I'd have to be shocked."

Mari flinched.

He rolled his shoulders, trying to ease the tension out of them. It had been a rough day, but he couldn't just spout off on this. It was obviously close to Mari's heart…and therefore, it would have to be handled delicately.

"Mari, it's not that I don't think they can handle it," he said gently. "I know they're good workers, and they're one of the best crews I've seen in a pinch." He wasn't lying. "And I know we've come up with some interesting stuff in the past. We've done well with it. But *Internationale is different.*"

She nodded, her gaze stony.

He hoped he was getting through to her. "They're the best, Mari. They're not going to be impressed with the stuff we put out. They're not going to appreciate it at all." He took a deep breath. "Maybe with a few wins from smaller competitions under our belt…more time to prepare…maybe…"

Maybe a name change, his subconscious traitorously added.

No matter what they did, he secretly felt that Guilty Pleasures would *never* win Internationale.

Mari sat on the edge of a large box of canned corn, and took a deep breath. "Did I ever tell you about my old restaurant? The one that reporter guy was talking about?"

Nick had forgotten the incident…largely because he'd focused on how upset Mari was, and on his feelings, both at David's stance on the article, and on David's confusing stance about Mari herself. "No. You mean…" What was it called again. "Le Pome, right?"

Suddenly, something that hadn't registered before flashed in his mind.

"Wait a minute," he said. "Le Pome. I know that…"

Not only that, but Phillip's comment about Mari being a failure linked together in his mind.

"You know." Mari's voice was flat. "I wondered when you'd put it together. I was only twenty-three years old when I was head chef of Le Pome. I was hand-picked by Derek Black, wealthy industrialist who wanted a restaurant. I thought he chose me because of my talent. Turns out, he chose me for my ass and my youth. And yes, I did sleep with him. I was stupid and young and flattered." She closed her eyes, her expression pained. "Did I mention I was stupid?"

Now it was Nick's turn to flinch.

"My parents were so proud…it was the first time they were *ever* proud of me. Derek was a friend of theirs, and they'd introduced us. They thought it was going to be the beginning of a really profitable partnership. Everything we bought was expensive—everything was tasteful. We had the most important interior designers, the best architect, the finest ingredients. And, of course, Derek brought every successful culinary consultant in to work on the menu. By the time we were ready to open, we invited every critic in the country, it seemed, to get a sneak preview of what would undoubtedly be the hottest restaurant on the West Coast.''

She looked away, like she was bored with the story, but Nick hung on every word. He knew what was going to happen next. Everyone in the culinary world knew the disaster that was Le Pome.

''I remember being in Derek's bed when I read the first review,'' she said, her voice dispassionate. ''How Le Pome was the biggest, most pretentious atrocity to hit the city in years. How it might be better if we got struck with a big earthquake than subject any patron to our boring, overengineered, overpriced slop.''

She obviously remembered every word…and he bet that she'd saved the more scathing reviews from that time. It had been a huge failure. Epic. He remembered it when he was working at the Four Seasons, how the owners had snickered over ''Derek Black's Folly,'' and ''that Worthington girl's career-ender.''

''Soon after, we couldn't get people in if we paid them. Derek started sniping at me. My parents wanted to know what I'd done. I tried changing things…fixing things…'' She shook her head. ''We closed our doors five months later. Four months after that, Derek had started bouncing on the aforementioned interior decorator and moving on to other pursuits. I was out of

a job, my reputation was a shambles, and my parents…well, disowned me. I was such a huge disgrace, and if I'd only listened to them and gotten my degree in business, none of this would have happened.…''
She took a deep, quavering breath. "Anyway, after that, I swore that I wouldn't let anybody let me feel that badly about myself again. So I worked hard, I saved. I had a trust fund coming. And when it came, I sank every last cent in my own restaurant, one that I wouldn't have to apologize or explain to *anybody.*''

She looked at him. "Do you know why I'm telling you this?"

He shook his head.

"Because the building's going under new ownership," she said quietly. "I need a mint in a hurry…my trust fund's all tied up and close to empty. Because Internationale is a long shot, but right now it's the only shot I can think of. Because I'm not ashamed of my restaurant, and because I believe we *can* win.''

She stopped, and he noticed that her eyes were bright with tears.

"Because I'm just now figuring out that you don't believe that.''

She turned, and before he could stop her, she walked through the kitchen and out the door.

7

MARI SAT AT LINDSAY'S house the following day. She had taken a day off, trusting Nick to open and close the restaurant, leaving the instructions on his answering machine. Yes, she was running away, and no, she wasn't proud. She had never trusted someone else to watch over the restaurant for a full day before. But as she'd told Lindsay, she hadn't taken sick leave from the restaurant the entire time they'd been open.

If ever a woman needed a mental health day, she had earned one.

She sat on Lindsay's couch, with a stoneware mug of green ginger tea, looking at the folder she'd pulled out from the recesses of her files.

Lindsay sat down next to her, looking at the clippings Mari had laid out. She made a small, sympathetic noise. "I thought you'd put this all behind you."

Mari looked over the newspaper articles and reviews. *Le Pome—Don't Waste Your Time; Derek Black's West Coast Disaster; Crashing and Burning at San Francisco's Le Pome.*

"I thought I'd put it all behind me, too," Mari said. "Apparently there's still a little bit left."

"You know, Nick was just being cautious," Lindsay said, her voice hesitant. "I don't think he was trying to be unsupportive. I mean, he might've chosen a better way to express it, but…"

She spread her hands helplessly.

"I know, Lindsay," Mari said. "I thought about that. Maybe I overreacted a little."

She could see Lindsay relax, but her friend still surveyed her warily.

"I just…I want somebody who believes in me, Lindsay," Mari said softly.

Lindsay looked pained. She didn't have a ready response for that, so she stood up. "You want some more tea?"

"No, I'm fine," Mari said with a smile. "Thanks for letting me crash over here."

"Anytime," Lindsay said. "My parents are looking at locations today, and I promised I'd help them. Are you going to be okay by yourself?"

"Sure," Mari answered. "Don't worry about me."

Lindsay obviously wasn't going to follow that bit of advice—worrying was in Lindsay's blood, Mari thought with a grin. "I'll be fine," Mari repeated.

Lindsay gave her a quick hug. "There's plenty of food in the fridge, and you can stay as long as you want," she said.

"I'll be out of here by tonight," Mari said, squeezing back in gratitude. "I'll give you a call if you're not back by the time I leave."

"All right." With that, Lindsay walked out of the apartment with a little wave.

Mari tried watching television, but nothing grabbed her…and the articles kept glaring at her. Finally, she gathered them up in a wad and walked out to Lindsay's balcony.

Lindsay had a gleaming red barbecue on the brick balcony…she didn't use it often, to Mari's knowledge, because she wasn't home much. But Mari felt sure Lindsay wouldn't mind it if she made use of it today.

She dumped the articles in the curved metal barbecue, pouring a little lighter fluid on top. Then she struck a long match and lit the edge of one review, watching blue flame crawl over it eagerly.

I'm not Marion Worthington anymore. Mari watched as the blaze grew, the paper blackening, the word disappearing. *I'm not that stupid girl. And I'm not going to keep reacting to something that happened years ago.*

That included how she was going to deal with Nick.

She'd still enter Internationale. She wasn't going to let the culinary world keep her down because she'd failed once. She had grown up. She had moved on.

Just let it go, Mari.

The smoke from the burning papers rose into the blue San Francisco sky, wafting off on the strong breeze. Mari felt her shoulders relax, for the first time in a long time.

When it had burned down to ash, she covered it, letting the charred remains cool. Then she walked back into the house. She sat down on the couch, and picked up Lindsay's phone, dialing Nick's home num-

ber with practiced ease. Her heart picked up its pace
a little, but she knew she'd get his answering machine.

"Nick? This is Mari." She took a deep, calming
breath. "I need to talk to you. Don't come to my
house…I want to meet you at the restaurant. I'll be
out for a while, so why don't you meet me there at
midnight? I'll talk to you then."

She hung up the phone, smiling. He hadn't been
trying to hurt her…and he hadn't been trying to *judge*
her. She knew that now. Just as she knew something
else—that he was the first man in a long time to actually try to protect her and help her out. That he was
the first man who she actually *trusted*.

She was going to show him that, she thought. Tonight.

IT WAS A SUNDAY NIGHT…they'd closed down at
nine. In the meantime, Nick had checked his phone
messages, hoping that Mari had called him so they
could talk. He didn't have Lindsay's number, and
even if he did… Well, it was obvious that Mari needed
some space, a little time.

Unfortunately, she *had* left a message…that she
wanted to meet him at the restaurant, not at her house.
That in itself boded ill, he thought. And she wanted
to meet him at midnight. That made no sense at all.

So now he was sitting in a booth at Tiger, the bar
the crew had been telling him about. He was sitting
next to Tiny, Zooey and Paulo, who had insisted they
come out with him. They didn't know about his midnight meeting with Mari. They didn't even know he

was on the outs with her. Or, technically, just how "in" with her he was.

He had a strong feeling that she was going to fire him. Or worse…tell him she wasn't going to see him again.

"Man, you've got to shake it off," Paulo said, motioning to the waitress. "Want another drink?"

Nick eyed the whisky sour in his hand. It was still half-full. "No, I'm fine." He wanted to be relatively quick-witted when he went to plead his case with Mari.

"You're not really fine," Zooey disagreed softly. He was actually surprised she was old enough to get into a bar. She looked at Tiny, who nodded.

"What's really going on?" Tiny said. "We're worried about Mari…and we get the feeling you know what's happened."

"You might've *been* what's happened, you know?" Paulo added.

Nick swirled his drink around, hearing the ice clink against the sides of the glass. Well, outside of Lindsay and Mo, these guys were the closest people in Mari's life. Maybe they could help him come up with a way to win her over. "Mari is mad at me. Because of Internationale." He grimaced. "Because of my *reaction* to her announcement that we'd be entering Internationale."

"Why?" Zooey asked.

"I didn't think we were ready for it," Nick said, then noticed their expressions. *Doesn't* anybody *at this restaurant believe in limitations? In taking things slow?* "That's not a reflection on you."

"It isn't, huh?" Tiny's expression was dark. "So what *you're* saying is, you're scared of bein' in the competition?"

Nick felt a flash of anger. "Of course not," he said, then realized how neatly he'd been trapped when the three of them responded with skeptical looks. "Okay. So maybe it was about you guys. Sort of. But it's not that I don't think you can do it. I just know what the competition's like. We're really inexperienced, comparatively."

"So what?" Paulo said. "Mari thinks we can make it. And just because we haven't been in a competition doesn't mean we can't, you know, *cook*."

"I know that," Nick said tiredly. "Believe me, I know. You guys are an incredible crew. But it's not just cooking at these things. You can't just be great. You have to be *perfect*. Dead on. Every time. One thing gets messed up, and you're history."

The three of them looked depressed at this. He felt like crap for bursting their bubble…almost as badly as when Mari stalked out of the restaurant, after dropping the bomb about her past on him. "I'm not saying it's impossible," he said.

"Come on," Paulo said, with a dismissive snort. "Don't try to blow sunshine, man. If we're gonna lose, just say so."

"There's a chance we could do well—a slim one, yeah—but if we come up with something really innovative…something that blows their socks off…."

He shrugged. "It'll have to be something they haven't seen before. Something really outstanding. We have to be ten times better than any of the other entrants."

Tiny looked at Paulo, who shook his head. Zooey, however, looked hopeful. "So if we just come up with something really wild and special, we can win it?" she reiterated, her face thoughtful.

Like that will be so easy, Nick thought, but nodded.

"All right. So we'll just work on that," Zooey said, her little face set with determination. She nudged Tiny. "Won't we?"

He smiled gently. "Sure, kid. We'll show 'em."

She smiled, then turned back to Nick. "And you'll patch things up with Mari, right?"

He took a deep breath. "That's going to be a little tougher," he said, thinking of his midnight appointment.

"Why?" she asked. "Because you're sleeping with her?"

Nick choked.

Paulo rolled his eyes. "Come on. Who doesn't know you two are doing the horizontal lambada?"

"We've known about it for months," Tiny said, with a booming laugh. "You two were being all secret-agent sneaky, thinking you were so cool about it. But that had to be the worst secret I've ever seen in my life. Even strangers would know you two were getting together after hours."

"How…what…" Nick floundered, feeling like an idiot.

"It's the way you *look* at her," Zooey said, grinning. "The way she looks at you."

"*Hot,*" Paulo said, with a wicked smirk. "Like you two just got naked before you walked into the room."

Nick felt heat bloom on his cheeks, and cursed himself. Dammit. He was actually *blushing.*

"She'll forgive you," Zooey said confidently. "Tell her you love her, and she'll lighten up."

Nick felt a strangling tension course through him.

When he didn't respond, Zooey's eyes narrowed. "You do love her, don't you? You've been together for *months.* You're crazy about each other."

Tiny nudged Zooey gently. "Honey, could you do me a favor? Go ask the bartender to set us up with another round."

Zooey looked ready to protest, but at Tiny's insistent look, she let out an impatient huff. "Okay. Be right back."

Tiny waited until she was out of earshot, then he and Paulo both turned to glare at Nick. "Zooey's a sweet kid, but sometimes, she doesn't know what's what. She's young, she thinks everybody's in love," Tiny said with a shrug of his massive shoulders. "Some of us know better."

Nick was still astounded at the turn the conversation had taken, and simply gaped at them.

"But some of us also know…you sleep with the boss, and you're asking for trouble," Paulo said. "We haven't said anything, 'cause Mari's a great woman and we figure, she knows what she's doing."

"But don't hurt her," Tiny said. "I don't care how you feel about her. If you're using her…"

"I'm not using her," Nick snapped.

Tiny smiled. "Okay, then. Then we'll be fine."

"I'm not going to hurt her," Nick said, feeling a burning in his chest. "I don't *want* to hurt her."

Tiny and Paulo fell silent, and Nick could feel them staring at him. "What?" he finally growled.

"You know," Tiny said. "The kid might be onto something."

"I don't know how I feel," Nick said. "Jeez. I never thought that this conversation would come up."

"Not with us," Paulo agreed. "But what are you gonna do when it comes up with, you know, *her?*"

Nick thought about it. "I don't know," he said softly.

Zooey came back, drinks in hand. "So. Did I miss anything?"

"Nah," Tiny said, taking his drink. "We just gave *jefe* here something to think about."

"So, when are you going to talk to Mari?" Zooey said brightly.

Nick glanced at his watch. It was eleven-fifty. "I guess I'll get going now."

"Good luck, man," Paulo said, putting his hand out. Nick slapped it.

"Yeah." Tiny said.

"She'll listen to you," Zooey said, with a smile.

"I hope so." Nick said, pulling on his coat and heading for the door.

That is, if she doesn't fire me first.

MARI SAT AT THE SMALL BAR in her restaurant. There were only a few small spotlights on, and the metal sliding doors had been shut in front of the large pane windows in the front, so the place was dark. Still, she admired the look of it…the rich colors, even in shadows, the set up of the tables. It was inviting, warm, beautiful. And it was the most important thing in her life.

Up to now.

"Mari? Hello?" She heard the back door open and shut, and Nick's voice calling from the kitchen. "Are you here?"

"In the front," she said, pulling her coat around herself a little more tightly.

He walked out through the swinging door, then stopped when he saw her. "Mari," he said.

She had deliberately positioned herself under one of the spotlights at the bar, and she smiled. "Sit with me," she said, with a gesture of invitation.

He walked to her, hesitantly, she noticed. He didn't look his confident self. His eyes burned as they traced over the contours of her trenchcoat, however, and she felt her body tingle.

"I know you're upset," Nick started. "So I want to explain a few things.…"

"Shh," she said, and glanced out at the darkened floor. "It's a beautiful restaurant, isn't it, Nick?"

He looked with her, and she could sense that he was puzzled, but he didn't want to show it. "Beautiful," he said, but when she looked at him, he was staring at her.

She warmed under his gaze. "I helped paint the

walls. I picked out all the furniture,'' she said. ''We had a limited budget, but it was *fun*. I fell in love with this place, Nick. I don't know that you'll ever understand how much this means to me.''

''I'm sorry,'' he said. ''I didn't mean to insult it. I wasn't trying—''

''I know,'' she said, cutting him off again. ''I know what you were trying to do.''

He got off the barstool, and leaned forward, enveloping her in his arms. ''If we've got no choice, then we're going to do it…and I'll do my damnedest to help you win.''

''This isn't about winning,'' she said, nudging him away. ''This isn't about the competition.''

She saw a ghost of nervousness cross his face. ''It's about us, then?''

She nodded.

He seemed to steel himself. ''I…''

She held a hand up to his lips, and she felt the faint brush of his mouth in a gentle kiss as his eyes closed.

Then she stood up, and she undid the belt of her trenchcoat, letting the whole thing drop to the floor. She was wearing a black teddy, black garter, stockings and black high heels.

''You may be wondering why I asked you here tonight,'' she said with a small grin as his eyes bulged.

''Um, yes,'' Nick said, in a strangled whisper. ''Although suddenly I'm in no rush.''

''I wanted to show you how much I cared about this restaurant. How important it was to me.'' She smiled. "And then show you how much I care about you."

He stood there, silent for a moment, and she saw emotions rush across his face...confusion, need, a sort of fragile happiness.

She opened her arms, and he reached for her.

"Mari," he growled against her skin, and she kissed him hungrily, feeling his hands stroke over the silk that covered her body, the slippery sensation making her hot. "I need you. I thought..."

"I know. I know," she whispered back. "I want to be with you. Now. Here."

He pulled away enough to look at her, then he undid his own coat and dropped it to the floor next to hers.

She closed her eyes as he ran his hands over her breasts, circling the sensitive nipples as she leaned back against the bar. She gripped at his forearms, feeling warmth and dampness start between her legs. "Nick," she breathed, rubbing against the denim of his jeans. "Please."

He sucked at her neck, and the slight pain of his kiss mingled with the pleasures of his touch. Her breathing accelerated and she brought one leg to rest on his hip, brushing herself against the erection she felt, long and hard. She let out a low moan as his hands moved lower, brushing at her clitoris through the silk. She felt the cloth move slick between her legs.

She had left a condom on the bar, and with trembling hands, she undid the button fly of his jeans, unzipping him slowly, enjoying the way his eyes closed. She nudged him to rest on the nearby barstool. She undid the snap on his boxers, and his erection emerged, hot and hard. She leaned down, letting her hair tickle him and relishing the moan he responded with. *This is what I wanted,* she thought. She took him in her mouth, taking as much of him in as she could, licking with abandon as she felt his hands bunch in her hair. She could feel his hips rock against her kiss, and after long moments, he tugged her away.

"Put it on," he said, his eyes bright gold in the light of the spotlight they were both in.

She smiled and sheathed him with the condom, then turned and leaned against the bar, shooting him a look over her shoulder.

He paused for a minute. "Are you sure?"

She nodded.

She held onto the bar as he walked behind her, pushing the thin strap of the teddy out of the way and gently pressing two fingers against her vagina. She arched her back as he felt her, stroking, stretching her slightly. She felt desire pulsing through her in waves. When he pressed against her, entering her with his cock, the brush of denim against the back of her thighs was enough to drive her crazy. He was hard and long and filled her completely, holding her breasts as he lowered her along his penis, pushing upward against her, sandwiching her to the bar.

"Nick," she breathed, as she felt the friction of him in a new way, one that excited her. She pushed against him as he rose to meet her, her breasts feeling heavy and hot as his hands played with her nipples. He pressed heated kisses on the back of her neck and shoulders, nipping at her until she thought she'd go mad with it. He plunged into her, and she bucked against him, breathing in harsh, panting breaths.

"Unh…yes…" he said, and he reached down with one hand to stroke along her clitoris, hitting her with a pleasure so close to pain it was overwhelming. They were mad with desire, moving as one in the spotlight of the darkened restaurant, pushing against each other as if they could by will alone become one person, one body.

"Nick, faster," she said, backing against him, the arch of her back and the press of her breasts against his hands almost forcing her to collapse.

He did as requested, and she felt the length of him withdraw almost completely, then ram home as one hand continued to stroke her breasts, the other her clit. She felt the stirrings of orgasm start up for her, and she cried out, bending like a bow against him. *"Nick!"*

"Yes," he yelled, and she felt him push against her, hard, causing her orgasm to echo and multiply. She shivered against him as she felt him empty himself into her, with a long, shuddering release.

They stood there for a second, propped against the bar, still joined, still feeling the sensual aftershocks. Her heart felt like it was ready to explode with what she was feeling.

"I love you, Nick," she said, in the silence that followed.

He didn't respond out loud, and for a second, her heart stilled, preparing for pain. Then he kissed her shoulders, easing out of her, and turned her around.

His eyes glowed.

"Take me home with you," he said. "And let me show you how I feel."

She smiled, and nodded, kissing him.

8

COULD THIS BE ANY MORE of a disaster?

Mari surveyed the kitchen, where it looked like Nick and the line cooks were all about to pull out knives and either battle each other with them, or fall on them and try to preserve their dignity. After her announcement—and subsequent explanation—about entering the Internationale competition, the crew and Nick agreed that they would work extra hours before work and on their Mondays off, trying to prep a menu and practice putting it together. The competition was now a little more than a month away.

She looked at the wreck of a rack-of-lamb in the middle station, the raging argument between Tiny and Nick, Paulo's heated discussion about the spicing of soup with Juan, and Zooey all but crying over the collapse of the soufflé she'd been experimenting with for a dessert.

Mari would have done better to set the kitchen on fire... But Jack MacDonald, or maybe the new owner, would be the one collecting the insurance, so *that* didn't help, either.

She knew she was pressuring herself, because she knew they didn't just have to be better than the rest…they had to be *stellar*. She and Nick were black sheep in the snow-white culinary community, and that would be a hard prejudice to beat.

Right now, they'd probably throw us out.

She heard a knocking at the door. Nobody else heard over the chaos, and Mari sighed. "I'll get it," she said.

She made her way through the infighting to the back door, opening it. It took her a second to register who was there, but when she did, she felt a smile burst across her face. *"Leon!"*

She threw a hug around her mentor. Suddenly, the tension of the morning—of the past two weeks—melted away. "I'm so glad to see you," she said, feeling the slight welling of tears despite her grin.

"I can see that," Leon said, in his dry, sardonic way. She could still hear the faint European accent that flavored his words. "Good God. Are these chefs, or a herd of elephants?"

"I'm *telling* you," Nick said to Tiny, "if we're going to do the lamb, we're going to need to get faster on those cuts!"

"And I'm tellin' *you,*" Tiny said, growling and plunking the knife down on the cutting board. "You ain't gonna *get* faster than that!"

Leon looked at Mari, and she cringed. "I see you're working on the Internationale menu," he said mildly, although the quirk of his eyebrow reminded her of school—just before he told a student to shape up, as she recalled. He walked over to the confrontation.

Nick took a look at Leon as he took a pause in

yelling with Tiny, looked away, then did a double take. "Leon?" he said, aghast. "I didn't know you were coming here!"

"Obviously." Leon's disapproval spoke volumes. He looked at the racks of lamb Tiny was systematically working on. "You're doing these French style, yes?"

Tiny nodded, still glaring at Nick. "Wonderboy here thinks I'm not going fast enough."

"If I might try?" Leon said, still in that mild voice.

Mari knew what was coming, and sidled up to the station to watch.

Tiny took a step back, taking in Leon's suit and fancy manner of speech. He gave a gesture of permission. "Whatever blows your hair back, pal."

Leon's lips quirked at the statement. He picked up Tiny's knife, frowning at the edge and taking a moment to sharpen it. Tiny rolled his eyes. "Oh, yeah, Nick," he muttered. "This is *much* faster."

Nick never stopped staring at Leon.

Leon closed his eyes for a moment, lamb in front of him, knife in hand. Then he got to work, quick slashes of the knife quickly stripping meat from the bones. With amazing rapidity, he had the lamb racked and "Frenched," the bones interlaced until they looked like a thatched roof.

"Not a neat job," Leon said critically, and Mari almost laughed at the look of astonishment on Tiny's face. "All the same...I think you'll find the technique a little, ah, *quicker.*"

"So you're, what, Superchef?" Tiny said, goggling at the perfectly presented lamb.

"I prefer the Lone Line Cook," Victor said, only the glint in his eyes betraying his sense of humor. "Off searching for kitchens in desperate need of my aid. And from the looks of you people, I seem to have arrived just in time."

Tiny, Zooey, Paulo and Juan were all staring now, at the strange older man with the dry smile and the lightning-fast knife. Nick smiled, hitching his thumbs on the top of his apron. "Leon. It's damned good to see you, old man."

"It's painful to see you," Leon said sharply, and Nick's grin broadened. "Did you forget *everything* I taught you?"

"No," Nick shot back, winking. "Just ignored it."

Leon tried glaring at him, but the smile and laugh won out. "A month to Internationale, your kitchen in a state of anarchy...and you still have time to mouth off."

Nick shrugged, but Mari could see the concern in his eyes. "You know we're going to compete, huh?"

"Mari called me and asked for my advice," Leon said, and although his voice was gruff, Mari could tell the warmth beneath the words. "The thought of my two favorite students in one of the most difficult culinary competitions in the world, without any of my input, was completely unacceptable. So I thought I'd butt in...in a consulting capacity, naturally."

Mari studied Nick's face. Ever since she'd seduced him at the bar, he'd thrown himself into prepping for the competition. They would go back to her place after a fourteen-hour day, sometimes ending with a quick bout of sex, always collapsing to sleep in each other's arms until the following morning. They hadn't spoken of his doubts or her declaration since, but she got the feeling that his dedication to the competition was, in a sense, a declaration back. So she wasn't sure how he would feel about her recruiting their school mentor…no matter how badly they were doing.

Nick frowned at first, then his gaze traveled around the kitchen, stopping on the soup, the lamb, Zooey's pancake-flat dessert.

"If you've got the time," Nick said, "I think we're open to suggestions."

Leon's eyes brightened, even though his expression didn't change. "Well. Why don't you show me the menu you've got?"

An hour later, Mari was popping aspirin and Nick was still scowling.

"Internationale isn't some state fair," Leon was saying, in his chef-as-drill-instructor voice. "What are you trying to say with these dishes?"

"It's called a sensual feast," Nick muttered, rubbing at his eyes. "So we want to offer as broad a palette of flavors as possible."

"That's not planning. That's shock value," Leon said, with a dismissive wave of his hand.

"You know," Tiny said, "I kinda thought that myself, but didn't want to say anything."

"So what are you saying?" Mari said. "We have to scrap *everything?*"

"Not quite," Leon said. "You just need to make it tighter. You need something to tie it all together."

Nick was growling now.

Leon shook his head. He looked at Tiny, Paulo, Juan and Zooey. "You haven't competed before, have you?"

They shook their heads. They were giving Leon the same deference that Mari had seen on the faces of every first-year student that had ever passed through Leon's cooking class. *He's right,* Mari thought, frowning.

"Tell you what," he said to Nick and Mari. "You two obviously need to work on this menu more. I've seen what you can do…the menu you've got for this restaurant is bold, exciting, and innovative. Whatever you did for that, you've got to do ten times as much for this, I want you two to go work on the menu." He turned to the rest of the crew. "In the meantime, I'm going to be teaching *you* lot some tricks of the trade. Before I'm done with you, you'll be more than ready to compete in Internationale…or anything else you decide to attempt."

Mari could have sworn they almost saluted him. She muffled a laugh.

"Take yourselves off, then," Leon said, his brow furrowing. "Be back by, say, seven. I'll take you to dinner myself. We'll see what you can come up with…and we'll talk strategy. Out!"

Nick looked at Mari, and she could tell he was feeling the same way…like a recalcitrant student, being told to go off and think about what she'd done. Nick took her hand, missing Leon's look of surprise. "C'mon, then," Nick whispered. "Let's see if we can't…ah, do what we did to come up with the first menu. Only ten times as much."

Mari smiled slowly. "Well," she said, looking away from Leon's querying gaze, "I suppose it wouldn't hurt to try."

NICK STRETCHED OUT on Mari's bed. He was more comfortable in it now than he was in his own bed…although any bed that Mari was in seemed like home, by this point.

She loves me.

She stretched out next to him, her hair loose. "I don't think that this is what Leon meant, exactly, do you?" she said with a mischievous grin.

"Well, he *did* say to do the same thing we did when we came up with the restaurant menu," Nick argued, stroking the back of Mari's neck and relishing her responding smile. "So it's not like we're ignoring his instructions."

"Small distinction," she said. "We're being *naughty.*"

He laughed, rolling her onto her back and nibbling at her neck. "So. Last time, we kicked around a couple of ideas, had sex like crazed rabbits, and…*voila.*" He wiggled his eyebrows. "So…what do you think? More of the same?"

He moved in to kiss her a little more seriously, and although his heart was in it, his body protested. After two weeks of backbreaking work, one part of his body was willing, but he hated to admit it...the rest of his muscles were weak. Well, maybe not *weak,* his masculine pride protested. But definitely *sore.*

When Mari laughed beneath his lips, he pulled away. "Tickle?"

"No," she said, giggling. "It's just..."

He hovered over her. "What?"

"Nick, love, I'm tired as all hell."

He burst into laughter, rolling onto his back. The two of them chuckled until they were breathless. Mari wiped at the tears that trickled from her eyes.

"I never thought I'd say that. Especially not about you," Mari said, gasping slightly. She trailed her fingers down his bare chest before resting her chin on it. "But man, these past few weeks have been a bear."

"I know, I know," Nick said, enjoying the viewpoint of her face gazing at his, the weight of her. He curved an arm around her, stroking absently at her soft skin. "I know I've only been at your restaurant for a few months...."

Mari closed her eyes for a minute. "Hmm. Four months now."

"Really?" He pushed the hair out of her eyes, brushing his fingertips along her jaw line after he tucked the stray strands behind her ear. "It just seems like longer, you know? Seems like..."

He didn't finish the sentence, but got the feeling she understood.

It seems like we've been together for a long, long time.

She nodded, kissing his abdomen. "You know, when I first met you, I thought…"

He tilted his head up, "Don't tell me. 'Who is this gorgeous, godlike man, and how can I get him in my bed?'"

"No," she replied, poking him in the ribs. "I thought, here comes trouble." She grinned. "The 'gorgeous-must-jump-him' part came later."

"I see." He pulled her until she was resting on top of him. "And do you still think I'm trouble?"

She nodded, and her violet gaze was warm, tender. "Yeah. But you're worth it."

"It's because of the sex, isn't it?" Nick said, meaning to joke. But for a second, he searched her face.

She loves me.

The weird thing was, he hadn't the foggiest idea *why*.

They'd had a chemistry so combustible it ought to carry a warning label. He knew himself—he had more than a streak of arrogance, what had been called a brutal ambition, a tendency to be bullheaded. He wasn't expressive. He wasn't sensitive. He wasn't really what any of those women's magazines said a woman wanted for anything other than a one-night stand.

She was staring at him, and he tried to play it off. "I mean, I pride myself on being creative in bed and all, so if you *are* in it just for the sex, hey, I don't think I can blame you.…"

"You know something? The sex is great, don't get

me wrong. Beyond great.'' She looked thoughtful. ''But what really got me was the food.''

''Huh?'' Her answer floored him. ''You mean...you love me because I'm good at my job?''

She leaned down and kissed him, and he could feel the tremors of laughter shaking her ribcage. When she pulled back, her eyes sparkled.

''No, you idiot,'' she said. ''Not how you cook. How much you love food.''

''Doesn't everyone?''

''Not everyone,'' she said, and rolled off of him, staring at the ceiling. He propped himself up on one arm, and contented himself with stroking the spot where her hip met her leg. ''My parents don't love food like that. They never really understood why I did. They'd say things like, 'Mari, why are you getting so involved in this? It's just *food*.' Like I was some bizarre sort of obsessive-compulsive. Like getting into culinary school was just something people who couldn't manage getting into a real college did.''

He shook his head, wanting to beat up the short-sighted people who obviously missed what was most special about their beautiful daughter. ''Well. They sound pretty...'' *Cruel*. He went for the safer description, one that would make her smile rather than remind her of the past. ''Square.''

''More like pretty status-conscious,'' she said. ''They thought the idea of their daughter being a cook was beneath them. In some ways, I think Derek did, too. He always introduced me as 'the only child of the Worthingtons' and *then* as the chef of his restaurant. Like it was my family connection that was much more important.'' She looked at him. ''You weren't like that. You really listened to me…even when I was coming up with really weird ideas.''

He closed his eyes and smiled. ''Like the circus menu.''

''God, yeah. That was a bad idea,'' she agreed. ''But you always listened. And you gave me chocolate instead of roses. And even though you thought we'd tank at Internationale, you still took it seriously. You never lied to me or put me down. You can even read my writing,'' she whispered. ''Sometimes I think you know me better after four months than most people have after years. And I feel like I know you.''

He nodded, pressing a tiny kiss against her shoulder. She was right. She seemed to be able to *read* him…the way he got angry, and she soothed him. The way she could coax him out of a creative block. The way she could turn him on with a smile and make him worry with a frown. The way she knew when he was hungry or when he needed something in the kitchen or just needed her to press her head against his chest or kiss him.

''What's the first food you can remember loving?'' he asked, against the choking of emotion in his throat.

''Ooh. A tough one,'' she said, with a smile. ''Hmm. I'd have to say chocolate chip cookies.'' She shrugged when he laughed. ''Hey, nobody's got a discerning palate at five.''

''No, no complaints. Like I said before, nothing's better than chocolate,'' he said, smiling. ''My mom was an incredible cook. She worked really hard in a kitchen all day, so you'd think she'd hate cooking, but she still did. When I'd come home from a really crappy day at school, she'd make me…'' He stopped. ''Never mind. You'll laugh.''

''No, really. I want to know.'' Mari nudged him, her eyes encouraging. ''What'd she make?''

''*Flan.* You know, custard. If I was really feeling lousy, she'd mix the eggs and the milk and then make the caramel, and pop it in a pan of water in the oven. I swear, I could eat an entire batch of it myself.'' He smiled. ''Come to think of it, I did.''

''That sounds nice.'' Mari sighed. ''For me—when I felt lousy, it was mashed potatoes. Or bread pudding.''

''If I aced a test—steak.'' His mouth watered just thinking of it. ''Or hand-rolled, deep-fried pork *flautas,* with the tortillas all crispy, and fresh guacamole…''

''Not for me,'' she replied with a smile. ''Celebrations were made for sushi.''

He laughed. ''Sort of made the jump from chocolate-chip cookies, huh?''

''It's funny,'' she mused. ''I think some of my best memories involve food.''

''Me, too.''

She sat up bolt upright in the bed. ''Wait a minute. That could be it.''

He stared at her. ''Huh?''

''Emotions and food. *That's* what'll give us an edge at the competition. Not a sensual feast,'' she said, leaning down and grabbing for a pad of paper at the edge of the bed. "An *emotional* feast."

"Mari, food is totally subjective," Nick said, still intrigued by the idea, but playing devil's advocate. "There's no way we can play on the heartstrings of complete strangers. It's not like we'll know their childhoods. They're all going to be different people. What's an experience they're all going to relate to?"

She frowned, still processing it. Then she smiled.

"Love," she said, and her eyes lit up. "They'll all have fallen in love, Nick."

He smiled. "So. You want to make a menu that's like falling in love?"

She nodded.

"Wow." He whistled. "You don't do anything half-measure, huh?"

"Think about it. Something exciting and dazzling to start…" She started doodling on the paper. "Something new and different and fun. Then something more mysterious and complicated, something more involving. Then move on to something warm and comforting and…" She gestured with the pen in her hand.

"Addicting?" Nick supplied, still staring at her.

"That's it. Something really compelling." She smiled. "Then the dessert would be something delicious, and still comforting and solid."

"Falling in love," Nick mused. Then he looked at Mari.

Her eyes were ablaze with creative energy, and there was a little half smile flirting with the corners of her mouth. She was focused on the paper, making her notations, brainstorming.

He kissed her, taking her attention away from her work for a second.

"What was that for?" she asked, and he was satisfied to see her focus blurring a little.

"For loving food," he said with a grin, then his tone grew more serious. "For loving *me,* Mari."

She dropped the paper and pen off the side of the bed, and reached for him.

"Maybe I'm not so tired after all," she whispered against his lips, and pulled him into her. "We can brainstorm a little bit later."

THEY WERE ONLY five minutes late to meet Leon at a little bistro he knew of, over in North Beach. The place was authentic Italian, not just the overhyped Italian designed to attract tourists. The three of them crammed into a little booth in the corner.

"I know the owner," Leon said, after being hugged by a huge man with a thick black beard.

"We gathered," Mari said, squeezing Nick's hand under the table.

"So. Do you have something to show me?"

Mari felt a little flutter of apprehension, until Nick stroked the nape of her neck and then draped his arm around her shoulders. She nodded and pulled out the sketches and descriptions from her purse, handing them over the table.

"I think you'll find it...." Mari took a deep breath. "Well, it'll be *different,* at any rate."

"Ringing endorsement," Leon said, but he smiled kindly anyway. "Let's see, then." He put a pair of wire-rimmed glasses on, picking up the paper.

"Relax," Nick whispered into her ear. "It'll be fine."

She leaned against him, reveling in his warmth, and she let some of the tension seep out of her. Still, she squirmed slightly, waiting for Leon's response.

He frowned, reading over everything carefully, going back to things. Nick squeezed her shoulders, and when she started tapping her foot against the metal leg of the table, Nick put his hand on her knee until she realized what she was doing and stopped.

"This," Leon said finally, "is unusual. Inspired. In short: it's pretty damned good."

Mari let out a breath and felt her spine slump. "Thank you," she said, then straightened, bracing herself for another onslaught. "But do you think it can *win?*"

Leon didn't say anything at first. Then, slowly, he smiled.

"Yes. If you can iron out the details, I think that it will be the freshest thing those tired old judges at Internationale have seen in years. I think you'll knock their proverbial socks off."

Mari leaned against Nick, and smiled when he brushed a kiss against her temple.

"But it's going to take a lot of work," Leon added. "I can work with your crew, but these appetizers are going to be time-consuming, and the main courses…"

"I'll worry about the main courses," Nick said.

"Of course, if you decide to throw any suggestions my way, I'm definitely open to them."

Leon nodded. Their waiter arrived, and they put in their orders. When he left, Nick looked at Mari.

"I'm going to wash my hands. Be right back."

She winked at him, watching him as he weaved his way between the tables.

"So." Leon sighed. "You're involved with Nick, then."

Mari looked at Leon. "Yes." She paused, feeling the weight of his stare. "You disapprove?"

"Well, moving past the idea of getting involved with someone you work with…" he said, and shook his head. "I care about Nick. I care about both of you. You were without a doubt two of my brightest students."

Mari warmed, smiling. "Thank you, Leon."

"But you were very different," he said, folding his hands together. "He's different, Mari."

"How do you mean?"

"He wants to be a success. More than he's wanted almost anything."

She tapped her fork against the table impatiently. "I don't mean to offend you, Leon, but I've heard this warning. From Lindsay…hell, from Nick himself. He's almost obsessively driven. But he *cares* about me."

"Yes, I know," Leon said. "That's what I'm worried about."

Mari blinked. "Pardon?"

"He obviously cares about you. Enough to drive

under his desire to have his own restaurant, and help you out. It may not be enough for him—but he's fighting it, to stay with you.''

She smiled. ''And that's wrong?''

''It will be if he learns to resent you for it.''

Mari took a sip of her water, thinking over his words.

Leon took a look at the bathroom, where Nick was emerging from the door. ''Mari, Nick is very intense. I know that he'll do anything to get what he wants. Including give up his dreams if he has to. But I'm afraid that a choice of that magnitude would tear him apart. Do you understand that?''

Mari nodded slowly.

''Just consider what might happen.''

''Back again,'' Nick said, sitting down next to Mari. His eyes glowed golden as he surveyed her. ''Well, you two are awfully serious. What've you been talking about while I was gone?''

Mari looked at Leon, whose face had gone back to a placid mask. ''Just the competition,'' Leon said easily. ''This isn't going to be an easy victory by any stretch. Are you sure you're dedicated enough to pull this off?''

Nick didn't stop looking at Mari. ''Yes,'' he said, in a low voice. ''I'm sure.''

Mari smiled back at him, but in the back of her mind, she felt a little twinge of doubt.

I'm afraid that a choice of that magnitude would tear him apart.

They had a chance at winning. Wouldn't Nick *want*

to stay at a top-ranked restaurant? With a new cash flow and a new building owner, the restaurant could be improved as the neighborhood was revitalized. She'd make sure that Nick got some publicity, he would have more than earned it. Would he really need his name over the door to be happy?

Would you be satisfied giving up your *restaurant to be with him?*

She frowned unhappily.

Nick kissed her. "Relax," he said smoothly. "It'll be all right."

She smiled back at him. *God, I hope so.*

9

IT WAS ONE WEEK TO Internationale. The crew had been working like fiends for the past few weeks, and the excitement and consequent tension was driving them all a little crazy. Leon had suggested that they all take a step away from the work, get some perspective…and some relaxation. Tiny and Paulo were playing basketball to work off the nerves. Zooey was apparently going to some kind of Tai Chi lesson ''to try to get the Zen of pastries,'' she'd claimed. Nick was out… He'd said at the movies, but she doubted he'd sit still that long.

Mari sat at a broad cherry conference room table in a posh office in downtown San Francisco. Lindsay looked cool as a cucumber in her pale green suit, her blonde hair swept up in a French twist that made her look like something out of a forties movie. Mari was glad she looked so collected. She, herself, was wearing a pinstripe suit that she hated, in air that felt sterile and sluggish, waiting for the new owner from this ''conglomerate'' to get in here.

Everybody else got to relax, Mari thought grumpily. *Why do I have to get stuck with this crap? Why can't I go play, too?*

She sighed, answering her own question. Because she was the owner. That brought responsibility. That changed the rules. Besides, winning Internationale wouldn't change anything if she got evicted the next day.

The door opened, and a tall, tanned man with pale blond hair stepped in. "Ladies. I'm sorry for keeping you waiting."

"Not at all," Lindsay said, standing and holding out her hand. "I'm Lindsay Everett, and this is the restaurant's owner, Mari Salazar."

"Ms. Salazar," he said smoothly, shaking her hand. "A pleasure, no pun intended. I've read a lot about you and your restaurant."

"Thanks." Mari smiled. "I'm sorry, your name is…?"

"Of course. Thoughtless of me." He sat down opposite them. "My name is Phillip Marceau."

Lindsay's eyes widened. Mari got to her feet.

"Come on, Lindsay," she said, her voice tight. "We're leaving."

"That's a trifle rude, don't you think?" Phillip's voice was cultured and mocking. "After all, I *do* own your building now."

Mari spun. "And now I see why. What is your *problem?* Nick didn't do anything to you."

"I suppose you'd think that. And I suppose you'd believe it." He didn't look so smooth now. There was a definite ferocity in his eyes. "I thought he was my friend. I thought he cared about me. But…well, all's fair in friendship and business, I suppose."

"Which is why you framed him for theft and embezzlement and then fired him," Mari snapped.

Lindsay stood at this, walking to stand next to Mari. "I don't think we should say anything else," she said, her voice low and quick. "Come on."

"I don't think you should leave just yet, Mari," Phillip interrupted.

"What the hell could you possibly have to say to me?"

"I have a deal for you." He pointed at Lindsay. "Just between you and me."

"We're leaving," Lindsay said, but Mari shook her head.

"Lin, wait for me outside, please?" She glared at Phillip. "I want to hear what Mr. Marceau thinks he can offer me."

"Isn't it obvious?" Lindsay whispered back. "He's going to threaten the restaurant because he's the new owner unless you pull out of the competition. Let's get out of here. I know a lawyer...."

"Oh, I don't think you've got the time or the money to go up against the Marceau family lawyers, dear Ms. Everett," Phillip said, his voice amused. "Fine. Mari, your friend has the gist of it, anyway."

"That's it?" Mari laughed. "That's so...*stereotypical.*"

He shrugged, his hands spread. "As Nick has often said, creativity is not my strong suit."

"But Nick is creative. Really creative." Mari shook her head. "You are pathetic, you know that? You're willing to screw up his career, just because you're jealous that he's talented and you're not?''

"It's not that simple," Phillip said, cultured tones slipping into a half-growl. "But I don't need to explain it to you. The bottom line is, I don't want him to be a success. And you can help me…or you can lose your restaurant. It's that simple."

"Or we can win," Mari replied, "and then I won't *need* your building."

"Oh, come on," he said, with a snicker. "One hundred and fifty grand in San Francisco? That won't get you a parking lot, and we both know it."

"There are investors…"

"That I can guarantee won't touch you if I tell them not to," Phillip said evenly.

Mari glanced at Lindsay, who was staring at Phillip in horror.

"You're a real bastard, aren't you?" Mari murmured.

"As you like."

"I don't like. One bit." Mari turned to Lindsay. "Come on. You're right…we should've just left."

"It's just a competition," Phillip said. "You skip this, I'll make sure that your rent stays the same for the next three years. Keep Nick buried in the Mission District, if you like. Keep on making raunchy entrees and pornographic desserts. But *keep him out of Internationale.*"

Before Mari could respond, Lindsay's eyes narrowed. "And you'd put that in writing?"

Mari gaped.

Phillip grinned. "Hmm. Perhaps I should've dealt directly with you."

"It's not her decision to make," Mari bit out, and Lindsay looked surprised. "We're leaving. *Now.*"

Lindsay followed Mari into the elevator. After the doors closed, Mari didn't trust herself to speak, until Lindsay finally broke the silence.

"It's just one competition, Mari. One we've only got a long shot at winning, anyway."

"I can't believe you." Mari didn't even look at her. "I can't believe you'd even *think* of stooping to that."

"Mari, I love you. You know that," Lindsay said. "But the important part has always been *saving your restaurant.* This will ensure that, especially if we can get it in writing. Why risk a long shot that will only get you evicted and threaten any chance you have at an investor, when you can save the restaurant right here, right now?"

"Because I'm not giving in to that bastard," Mari said. "I'm not going to quit just because he feels…"

"You're not going to quit because it would hurt Nick." Lindsay's face was a mask of sadness. "Mari, you're so in love, it's making you blind. Ask him. See what choice he'd make. If he really wants to help your restaurant, then he'll back down. If he *doesn't* want to help, then he'll choose the competition."

"He'd never let Phillip do this to me."

"Like you said in the conference room," Lindsay said softly. "Honey, it's *your* decision to make."

Mari shook her head.

"I'm sorry," Lindsay said. "I know it seems

bitchy. But you're thinking with your heart, and it could cost you your restaurant. I'm not trying to hurt you. I know I'm not creative or free-spirited like you are, but I know my job. And that's watching your back.''

''I know,'' Mari said, her voice cracking. ''I know.''

They rode the elevator down to the lobby, and Mari took a deep breath when they finally made it out to the street.

''So. What are you going to do?'' Lindsay said nervously.

''I'm going to think.'' Mari sighed. ''And I'm going to talk to Nick.''

NICK WANDERED THROUGH the aisles of Whole Foods Market, breathing in the scents of aged cheese, fresh produce, bakery-warm breads and baguettes. Here he was, supposed to be relaxing…and back in his interminable search for food to experiment with.

He grinned. He'd told Mari he was going to see a movie. He could tell from the smirk she gave him before she left that she knew better.

What really got me was the food…the way you love food.

He smiled to himself, tasting a sample of goat cheese on papery-dry wheat crackers. He'd dated other chefs before, but he'd never met one that matched his desires, and understood him, as well as Mari did.

''Nick? Hello. Earth to Nick.''

He turned. ''Hmm?''

It was Bob Blackstone, grinning with that slight nervous edge that he always seemed to have. ''I've been trying to say hello to you for the past five minutes,'' he said with a low laugh. ''Thought you were dogging me.''

''Sorry.'' Nick shrugged. ''I just have a lot on my mind lately. So, how are…''

''I'll bet,'' Bob said with feeling. ''What with Internationale and all.''

''You know that we're competing, too, huh?'' Nick shook his head. ''What, are we at the top of the list or something?''

''Come on, Nick.'' Now Bob's eyes were shrewd. Funny, that Nick hadn't noticed that before, back when he'd worked for him, so long ago. ''I couldn't believe it when I saw your restaurant in the *Chronicle,* then in *S. F. Food & Wine…* I have to say, I didn't think anybody could pull that stunt off.'' He shook his head, laughing a little stronger now. Sales-friendly laughter, Nick thought, not joining in. ''I should have known that you could, Nick. Damn! And now you're going to be in Internationale with that bunch!''

''That 'bunch' is a great crew,'' Nick said, clamping down on the sudden burst of temper that flashed through him. ''They've worked really hard.''

Bob obviously knew that he'd mis-stepped, and backtracked. ''Well, you could whip any team into shape, Nick.''

Nick's eyes narrowed. ''What do you want, Bob?''

Bob looked offended for a moment, then his posture deflated. ''Blackstone's isn't doing as well as it was.

What restaurant is in this economy, huh?'' He sighed. ''Only the top places with the showiest chefs seem to make it anymore. Like you've got to have a show on the Food Network to make any kind of money.'' His voice was rich with contempt.

''I'm sorry to hear that,'' Nick said, and he meant it.

''You've been insane about this industry since I met you, Nick,'' Bob said, his voice a little lower now. ''You could make something out of nothing. I decided to let you make your chops with Four Seasons, then, when you were ready, I thought I'd bring you on. But Marceau beat me to it. Who can go up against those guys?''

''You could have hired me four months ago,'' Nick pointed out. ''Without competition, as I recall.''

Bob looked uncomfortable, shifting his weight from foot to foot. ''Well, that was different.''

Nick shrugged. ''Whatever eases your conscience, I suppose.''

He turned to leave, but Bob stepped in front of him. ''Hear me out,'' he said. ''Yeah, well, I probably should have trusted you, but...well, you *know* why.'' His voice was urgent, just this side of frantic. ''Now, you're starting to get your rep back...small press, yeah, but still *press,* all for a little bupkis restaurant in the middle of a war zone. You win Internationale, and you'll be able to write your own ticket.''

Nick looked at him, bewildered, when suddenly it struck him.

He thinks we'll win.

"I want Blackstone's to be that ticket," Bob said. "You win Internationale, and I'll make sure not only is your name on the menu, but you'll get the biggest press push you've ever seen. Hell. *I'll* get you on the Food Network. How does that sound?"

"How about changing the name to...I don't know. 'Nick's' or something?"

Bob goggled.

Nick laughed. "Sorry, Bob. I'm not interested. I want to build something of my own. And I don't need your help or your gracious offer...but thanks anyway."

He walked away with Bob still goggling.

Nick walked out to his car, mulling it over.

You win Internationale, and you'll be able to write your own ticket.

He hadn't thought about it that way. Internationale was a way of trying to help Mari...help the restaurant, the crew, make it. He hadn't thought they had a snowball's chance in hell in winning at first, then he'd grown cautiously optimistic, but obviously there was buzz. Bob knew it. If Bob knew it, then other people were talking about it.

We might win.

All Nick had wanted was to build his reputation back, and get a restaurant of his own. Then he'd gone to work for Guilty Pleasures, gotten involved with Mari Salazar, and his whole world had turned upside. Now, he wasn't sure what he wanted...or if he could have everything he wanted.

We might win.

But what would he be winning? And, if he wrote his own ticket…what might he be losing?

He needed to think this through. Talk this out.

Instinctively, the only person he wanted to talk to about this was Mari…and she was the very cause of the conflict in the first place. If he hadn't met her…if he hadn't fallen in love with her…

He almost slammed on the brakes.

Of course you're in love with her, idiot.

He knew he cared about her. It wasn't until now, when he had the chance of getting out of Guilty Pleasures and back on track, that he realized how much. He wasn't going to keep climbing up the ladder toward a dream that might or might not happen and hurt her along the way.

I love her.

He drove toward her house. He would wait for her to get back from her meeting.

Then he'd tell her what he felt sure she already knew.

10

MARI WALKED UP TO her apartment with a sense of doom.

I don't want to have this conversation.

She didn't know which would be worse…telling Nick that the guy who'd ruined his reputation in the first place was now going after him at Guilty Pleasures, or telling him that his decision to knuckle under to Phillip's demands might be the only thing that saved her beloved restaurant.

She unlocked the door, and opened it.

There were flowers everywhere, it seemed, she thought as she looked around. Deep violet irises, large white lilies, fragrant freesia and lots of other blossoms she didn't even know the names of. It was like a garden in her loft.

"Was wondering when you were going to get back from your meeting," Nick said, grinning.

"What's the occasion?" Mari said, momentarily floored.

He walked up to her, kissing her lightly. "You are," he murmured, taking her purse and putting it down on the kitchen table. "See what I've got for you."

He walked her to the kitchen, and pulled a covered tray out of the fridge. He lifted off the top.

"Sushi," she said, dazzled by the sheer variety he'd picked up.

"The only way to celebrate, remember?" A timer went off, and he put the tray of sushi down on a nearby counter. "Wait a sec."

She inhaled deeply, trying to get her bearings. This was not making things any easier...but she was touched, nonetheless.

He opened the oven, revealing a pan full of choc-olate-chip cookies, and her eyes misted.

"So...am I the celebration, too?" Mari said around the lump in her throat.

"Sort of." He put the pan down on the stove. "Come here a sec."

She walked into his arms, and looked into his now-serious eyes.

"I did a lot of thinking today, while I was out." He smiled sheepishly. "I, ah, didn't go to the movies. I went to Whole Foods instead."

She laughed, despite her nerves. It was just so *him*.

"Anyway, I thought about us. About our conver-sation about loving food. Why we loved it, what we loved best. And I figured out something that I should've been more attuned to before, if I weren't so... Well, if I'd been paying attention."

"And that is...?"

"That I love food," he said, kissing her. "But I love you more, Mari."

That did it. Tears crawled down her cheeks, and she

closed her eyes, tasting the salt of them mingling with his kisses.

"Took you long enough," she said, when he tucked her head under his chin and held her tight.

"Well, I threw a little party for you to make up for it," he said, and she let out a watery giggle. "That's got to count for something."

"You always think of me," she said, hugging him fiercely.

How can I tell you what happened now? After all this?

"This way. Let's eat," he said, setting the food on the table. They both sat down. "I figured you'd be hungry—and stressed—after the talk with the new owner. How did that go, anyway?"

She tensed. This was the moment.

"He…" She swallowed hard, chickening out. "I'm trying not to think worst case scenario, but it doesn't look good."

"What does he want?"

He wants us to pull out of Internationale.

"He was just trying to be a hard-ass," Mari said instead. "I think he'll probably want us to move."

Nick's brow furrowed. "No way to talk him out of it, huh?"

"No way to reason with the guy. I guess I'll probably get evicted."

Nick reached out, held her hand. "Maybe it won't get that bad. Anything I can do?"

"Probably not." *Except…* "Nick, can I ask you a question?"

He smiled.

"Do you still think Internationale is a good idea? I mean, you were against it from the start...." She picked up some sushi, put it down on her plate more to give her hands something to do—and to avoid his probing gaze. "What if we dropped out? I'd lose some deposit money, but..."

"Mari, I know how much my doubting hurt you. I guess I was scared. But after working with your crew and Leon, and after all we've come up with—I *know* we've got a shot at winning. I believe in us. Now, I *want* to compete. I know we can win, Mari. I can feel it."

She could hear the sincerity ringing in every word. "One other question," she said slowly. "Phillip's in Internationale, right? What would you do if he...you know...wins? If he beats us?"

"Then he'll pull off a miracle," Nick said, his face darkening momentarily. "But the bottom line here isn't Phillip, anyway. It's not even about me. This is for you...and your restaurant."

He looked out the window a minute, pensively, then turned back. "Besides, I'm not going to let the threat of Phillip hang over my head for the rest of my life. Since I've met you, I've got better things to think about."

His words galvanized her.

If I give in to Phillip, I'll have to live with his black-mail for the rest of my life...anything I do will be dictated by whether or not he'll evict me. And he'll keep on hurting Nick, given the chance.

Nick was right. She had better things to think about than Phillip Marceau.

"You okay?" Nick said, stroking her cheek.

"I'm fine," Mari said. "I just want to focus on the competition from here on out."

IT WAS FINALLY HERE…Internationale, the day of the competition. It was seven o'clock in the morning, in a huge auditorium, just off of San Francisco's Union Square. Crews from various restaurants, hard to distinguish in their almost identical chef's whites, were scrambling to set up in the small, stainless steel "stations" that were designated to each six-person. Each team would have two relatively small ovens, a refrigerator–freezer, a set of four burners, counter space for portable fryers or any other tools they chose to bring. They would have five hours when the competition officially started at nine that morning. They would need to be prepped, with all of their ingredients ready, by nine…but no ovens or burners were to be turned on until that time.

Mari smiled as Tiny, Paulo, Zooey and Juan craned their heads this way and that, taking in the bursts of French and German and Spanish from all the other teams. They themselves were wearing their usual—black long-sleeved T-shirts, black aprons, black loose-fitting pants.

They looked like ninjas at a karate exposition, Mari thought with a low laugh. Well, she was okay with standing out.

If we're going out, we're going out with a bang.

Nick was hyper, she noticed…bordering on manic. He logged all the ingredients on his checklist, clicking the ballpoint pen open and shut with his thumb.

"Okay…Meyer lemons, we've got the pork, we've got the makings for the appetizers…wait a minute. Where's the Phyllo dough?" He started rooting around in the boxes. "Tell me we didn't forget the Phyllo!"

"Got it here, boss," Tiny said, rolling his eyes at Mari. He leaned over and whispered to her, "Is he always like this?"

"I have no idea," Mari thought. But she had an inkling of *why* he was being this crazed.

He wanted to win. Not just for himself—for *her*. And consequently, he was going a little nuts.

"Can't you talk to him?" Zooey said plaintively half an hour later, after Nick moved things around for the third time and compulsively gone over his list for a seventh time. They were early into their competition booth, set up, watching the other teams get ready. The waiting was grating on all of them.

Mari walked over to Nick, who was muttering to himself. "You okay?"

"Huh?" Nick looked at her, obviously not seeing her but still focused on whatever it was he was concentrating on. "Sorry. Yeah, sure. We'll be fine. I just want to make sure everything's ready to go."

"You've 'made sure' to the point of paranoia, Nick," Mari said with a small grin. "Let's go. Walk with me."

She noticed Paulo, Tiny, Juan and Zooey heaving

sighs of relief as she guided Nick out to a side hallway that led to the basement of the auditorium, away from the traffic and bustle of the other competitors. ''I've never seen you this...'' she searched for a word ''....unglued. What's up?''

He shook his head. ''Sorry. I should've warned you...I didn't think about it until this morning.''

''What?'' she said, feeling a queasy sort of nervousness rise in her throat.

''I'm a basket case on competition days,'' he said, and his tone actually made her laugh. ''I'm serious. When I competed in Internationale last time, my teammates threatened to tie me up and stuff me in a broom closet until the thing actually started. I just get a little keyed up before events, that's all. Nervous energy.''

Energy was right—she could feel it crackling from him, like static electricity. She could understand it, because she was feeling the same burst of nervous energy herself. Only, knowing that it was certain death for her restaurant, she could put more emphasis on the ''nervous'' part.

He needed a distraction, obviously, she thought. They both did. The next couple of hours would be brutal, and the judging... She didn't even want to *think* about that.

So what could distract them both for a while, take them away from all this?

She saw a door slightly ajar down the dusty hallway. In the slight light from the hallway, she thought she could make out brooms and mops. She grinned.

"This way," she said, tugging his hand. "I've got an idea."

She pushed open the door, taking a minute to find the light switch, which lit a single naked bulb hanging from the ceiling. It was a utility closet of some sort. There were various props from the theater works that were performed in the auditorium, some music stands, some cabinets, as well as various cleaning supplies. She pulled him in, tested the doorknob, and then shut the door.

He looked at her, quirking an eyebrow curiously. "What?"

"Well, I won't tie you up," she said, smiling slowly. "But I can keep you in here until the competition starts."

He laughed, until she walked up to him, tracing the fly of his jeans, stroking the bulge underneath until he groaned and started growing hard. Then she got up on her toes, kissing him slowly, her tongue teasing his lips until his tongue met hers.

He pulled away, his breathing short. "Mari, this is crazy. There's sixty teams out there, all getting their game plan on…"

"This is how we started things," she said, unbuttoning her own pants and pulling the zipper down, watching his eyes widen and then move toward the door. "I think that *this* is our game plan."

He smiled, stroking her chest before trying to stop her fingers from removing her pants. "I hate to remind you, but there are some of the world's top food journalists and renowned chefs out there waiting to judge us.'' He kissed her neck, his words full of reluctance. ''What would they do if they found out one of their competing teams was off having a quickie in a broom closet?''

''Envy us,'' she said with a smile, kicking off her shoes and tugging her loose-fitting pants down the rest of the way, until she was standing in bikini panties. ''Besides, it's not going to be that quick.''

Nick smiled, then closed his eyes and let her undo his pants, tugging them over his perfect behind. He kicked off his own shoes and left his pants on the floor.

''I can't believe we're doing this,'' he said, and she could hear the grin in his voice…as well as the excitement. She could also feel the bulge of his erection straining against the thin cotton of his boxers. ''Hell, Mari. Somebody could walk in, find us…''

''I know,'' she whispered. Then she smiled and wiggled her eyebrows.

He laughed, as she'd hoped.

She leaned back against a wall, and motioned to him. He walked to her, kissing her slowly, their lips brushing against each other as his fingers smoothed themselves over her shirt. She tugged it over her head, putting it on a nearby pedestal. Now she was just in her underwear, the cool basement air in the room making her skin prickle.

He kissed her shoulders, rubbing fingers over her rib cage as she tugged at his shirt and put it by her own. He pressed against her, his skin warm compared to the cool air, and she brushed against him, moaning.

Soon, their kisses grew more urgent, as she brushed her panties against his boxers, feeling them dampen, feeling him grow even harder until he was prodding at the juncture of her thighs. He pressed against her in a mimicking action of their lovemaking, and she let out a sighing breath, tilting her head back as he kissed her jawline, and the sensitive hollow behind her ears.

"Mari," he breathed. Then he paused. "Sudden, dreadful realization—I don't have any, er, protection on me."

"Condom," she said. "In my pants pocket."

He broke away from her long enough to get it out of her pocket, then handed it to her. "So. You planned this?" he said with a grin, his eyes hot and full of desire.

"You've got your checklists," she said, panting as she tugged the thing open and he slipped out of his boxers. "I've got mine."

He chuckled, putting the condom on as she slid off her panties and unclasped her bra. She could barely hear the rumbling din of set up as the teams took their places upstairs.

Right now, out there wasn't important. What happened to her restaurant wasn't important. The only thing that mattered at this moment was the man standing in front of her. "Lift me up," she murmured.

He obliged her, lifting her up slightly, propping her against the wall as he angled himself at her entrance. His muscles bulged and flexed with the effort, and his face was tight with concentration. His eyes were dilated, their whisky color now almost entirely black.

The lightbulb swung slightly, adding to the surreal effect. She felt him, huge and probing, in between the delicate flesh of her thighs. She leaned her head back against the wall and tucked her legs around his hips as he lowered her onto his erection. She moaned, feeling him inch by unyielding inch.

"You feel incredible," he whispered, as he moved his hips and legs to press inside her more deeply. She rotated her hips slightly, enjoying his responding shudder as well as her own sensual shivers. He kissed her slowly, his tongue corresponding with the actions of his lower body, dipping inside her, tasting her, teasing her. She tasted him as well, as her body clenched against his.

He lifted her legs a little, changing the angle of his entry. He started pushing against her, and she felt the brush of his penis against her clit as he slid out then returned, a steady rhythm, increasing in pressure. His chest was crushed against her breasts, and the wall felt cold against her backside in contrast with the inferno sliding against her. *Inside* of her.

She could feel the beat of his heart as she clutched at the back of his neck, at the firm muscles of his shoulders. He picked up in speed, and she tightened her thighs around him, trying to get as much of him in as possible as his hands clutched at her hips and pulled her to him. They were moving faster now, causing the waves of sensation to double, pulsing through her chest, making her nipples erect. "I'm close," she gasped against his ear.

To her delight, he angled her so that he was brushing against her clit, making that pleasure center bloom with heat and friction, an explosion of sensation. "Ah…*ah*…" she breathed against him, moving her hips, slamming against him as the waves of orgasm rolled against her. *"Nick!"* she cried, the sound muted as he covered her mouth with his own and moved up inside her, his cock stroking against her relentlessly.

"Yes," he said, now her mouth muting the sounds, as he shuddered against her, the resounding pressure of his thrust causing her own waning orgasm to burst back into life. She cried out, her arms and legs wrapped around him like a vise.

She might have passed out, she wasn't sure. When she blinked long moments after, her breathing slowly getting back to normal, he was practically crushing her against the wall.

"Nick," she said, stroking at his sweat-damp neck. "Nick, I love you."

His arms tightened imperceptibly around her. "I love you too, Mari," he answered, and she felt the thrill of his response like it was the first time he'd said it. "More than I thought I'd love anyone."

He eased her to the floor, and as he withdrew she felt his absence as keenly as pain. "So. I guess it's time to go back out there," she said slowly, hating the fact that they'd have to go back to the competition, to the possible failure of her restaurant…to all that *reality.*

He smiled, and to her surprise, he kissed her. "You know," he said slowly, "we've still got about half an hour."

''I see.''

''It'll help us to get ready.''

She rifled through her pockets for another condom, then held it up. ''You sure, cowboy?'' she said, winking. ''I mean, I don't want you to be all tired out.''

His grin was fierce. ''Give me a few minutes to recover,'' he said, ''and we'll see who's tired.''

NICK WAS STILL GRINNING as the competition commenced. They were an hour in, and working busily. He couldn't remember being this loose or relaxed at a competition, ever. He felt pretty sure that Paulo, Tiny and Juan figured out what had happened, from the way they were grinning back at him. Zooey was working industriously on the Pot of Chocolate for the dessert, so he doubted that she knew that her head chef and sous-chef had just gotten it on in a utility closet.

He glanced over to where Mari was working on the flashy appetizers, and saw that she had a hickey on her neck…one she didn't have when they walked in that morning.

Well, if anybody didn't know, I guess they'd put it together soon enough.

But he didn't even care about that. The clock was running, the whole auditorium a flurry of movement and yelling in several languages as the ''foodie'' crowd of spectators and restaurant investors milled around and gawked. Photographers from different trade journals and newspapers snapped bright flash photos. It was distracting and unnerving to some, but Nick was thriving on it.

"Nick! Nick Avery!"

He smiled at the reporter yelling at him. The guy looked familiar, but he didn't remember his name. "Little busy here," Nick drawled, as he cut succulent pork rounds and marinated them.

"What's with the black clothing? Is it some kind of statement?" The reporter pressed. "And what have you got planned?"

"We like wearing what we're comfortable in," Nick said. "And you know I'm not going to tell you what we've got planned. You'll find out when the judges do."

A couple of other reporters stepped up and started hounding him. "What happened at Le Chapeau Noir? Is this a grudge match? Can you beat Phillip Marceau?"

Now Nick was getting annoyed. "No, it's not a grudge match. I wanted a change. Chapeau's got nothing to entice me anymore." Even as he said the words, he realized they were true. "I'm being ten times more creative and allowed more freedoms now than I ever have. I'm having more fun, too."

"Don't you miss it, though?" The first reporter was particularly persistent…reminding him of David's questions. "Being in a four-star restaurant, being at the top of the culinary world?"

Nick laughed. "What makes you think I won't be after today?"

The reporters laughed with him, and he felt relieved...until the guy's next question.

"So...you're not going to leave this restaurant, *Guilty Pleasures,* if you win, huh? Is that what you're saying?"

That quieted the rest of them, as they waited, poised to jot down his answer.

He hadn't thought about it. Had tried desperately hard *not* to think about it, since Bob Blackstone's proposition in Whole Foods Market.

"I doubt it," he said, hating even that hint of uncertainty. "Put it this way...I'd have to be offered a hell of a lot more than just a head chef's position. If I had an unlimited budget, my own restaurant, and...I don't know, the keys to a Lexus or something, then I might *consider* it." He shook his head. "But I have to tell you...it'd be hard to top what I've got here."

They wrote hurriedly. Before they could ask some more questions, Mari moved forward.

"You're distracting my team," she told them, with a firm but friendly tone.

"Nick..."

"Move it," Mari added. Her gaze was like violet ice.

They got the hint and started pestering other stations. Nick looked down at Mari, who was staring at him warily.

"They're jackals," he said with a shrug. "When you're on the way down, they can't wait to nail the coffin shut. When you're on the way up, they want to act like they put you there. You remember that?"

"Yeah," she said. "I remember."

He leaned down and kissed her, causing Tiny and Paulo to whistle and getting some attention from the reporters, who snapped a shot. Mari flinched at the flash of light.

"Just worry about today, okay?" Nick said, ignoring everyone and every thing else.

She nodded slowly.

"All right then," he said, turning back to his work. "We've got a competition to win."

But he still thought about it.

Will I leave? I doubt it. I've got a woman who loves me, a restaurant I'm happy with, a nice life.

But he thought of what he'd gone through to get there.

I doubt it, he repeated to himself.

But as much as he loved Mari, there was still a shadow of doubt…and that really disturbed him.

THEY WERE GETTING CLOSE to the end, working on setting up the food on broad, mirror-surfaced platters that the competition's "waiters" would parade before the photographers and judges before plating and serving the entries. Mari felt like her shoulders were stapled together with the stress of working so hurriedly, of getting everything perfect. She jumped when Nick walked behind her, rubbing at the back of her neck. "It's almost over," he whispered in her ear.

That had two connotations in her mind—not that he knew that it. But it didn't help her tension much, either. Still, the feeling of his strong fingers massaging her was soothing, and she needed all the soothing she could get.

"Got it," Tiny said, letting out a breath. Everything was arranged artistically, and she had to admit, it looked fantastic. The "waiters," all dressed in tuxedoes, carried her food away, and she felt a pang of loss.

Did we do everything we possibly could? she asked herself feverishly. *Was everything right?*

She sank back, tapping her toes as the rest of the crew watched the parade of consumables. The rest of the dishes entered didn't take the same route they had, Mari noticed. There were the usual towers of potato gallettes, the same sautés, the same foie gras and black truffles. Theirs was next in line, and they waited like expectant parents. Mari felt Nick hold her hand, and she squeezed it tight.

"The next entry is from the restaurant, ah…" the commentator stumbled. "Guilty Pleasures."

There was a ragged cheer from the crowd, and Mari smiled.

"Their entry is called A Taste Of Love," he said, and she could have sworn she heard a tone of disapproval. "First, an opening aperitif of Kir Royales, titled 'First Date.' Opening appetizers are titled 'First Kiss,' comprised of chili and mango tarts. Fish dish is a form of sushi…"

Mari waited as he listed off the rest of the entrees, the different kinds of sushi they'd concocted, designed to surprise and tantalize…the savory pork cassoulet, meant to be savory and addictive. The Meyer lemon sorbet between courses as "the next level" palate cleanser. And finally the sweet smoothness of the Pot of Chocolate. If nothing else, it would probably wake up the deadened taste buds of a bored-looking judging panel…and remind them that food didn't have to be so painfully art-house, oversculpted, overengineered and overpriced.

From the smiles on several faces as they ate their portions, she had a real hope that they would get the point.

It was scary to hope, but they'd already accomplished more than she ever would have thought possible. At first, the other teams had been stand-offish, and she knew they didn't think much of the black-clad "Guilty Pleasures" group. Rather than being intimidated, the crew had approached the competition with a dogged determination, and best of all, with their trademark sense of humor. They'd laughed, sung, and in general made enough of a ruckus to earn the looks of censure from the gray-haired, pot-bellied head chefs from other restaurants…and, when the head chefs weren't looking, they'd gained the grins from other crews. When she'd discovered that the restaurant to their right had crushed a batch of eggs and lost a bottle of tarragon vinegar, she was thankful for Nick's over-zealous preparation, and had handed them over, much to Nick's surprise. News of her little charity was spreading—partly as a sign of respect, which made her happy. But also partly as a sign of her foolishness, which made her sad, not because other people thought her foolish, but because these people were so hell-bent on winning that they'd ignore the problems of the other teams. It seemed like a hell of a big prize to her—even if it wasn't enough to save her. But for some of the other teams, winning this was more than just the prize—it was driving the other teams into the ground. It was war.

"Jeez," Paulo said, staring at the judges as they scrutinized every bite. "You'd think they never ate mangoes before."

Nick laughed. "Don't worry. They do that to everybody. We did a hell of a good job today. I think we've garnered the attention of the culinary world, in fact." He was buoyant, she noticed, and felt her spirits lift a little. That is, until he added, "Don't be surprised if a bunch of restaurant people start giving you their card and trying to steal you away, guys."

That provoked a string of nervous laughter from the crew. "They'd have to cough up a hell of a lot of money," Tiny said, shaking his head.

Mari felt unnerved. Once the restaurant went under…well, maybe they wouldn't have to cough up that much money. And at least the crew would have jobs, right?

She pushed herself away from the countertop she was leaning on. "I have to take a walk, get some fresh air…something," Mari said.

Nick stopped her, nudging her chin up so her eyes met his. "You okay?" he asked, in a low voice. "Want me to come with you?"

"No, that's all right," she said, thinking *I want you*

to remind me that this was the right choice. "I'll be right back."

She walked down the main corridor, toward the doors that led to the bright sunshine outside. She saw that there were several chefs already beyond the front door, puffing away at cigarettes and talking amongst each other. She didn't feel up to facing them, and that wasn't the freshest air she could find. She glanced down an adjoining hallway and saw an open window. She made her way over to it, breathing in the cooling air. It was afternoon. They were one of the last teams to go through judging. An hour, tops, and it would all be over.

She thought back on her restaurant—of everything she'd put into it.

It'll all be over.

"Mari."

She turned. "Phillip Marceau," she said, her voice tight. "To make my afternoon complete, I saw your entry." She suppressed the urge to roll her eyes. "Very artistic." Actually, it was ludicrous; there were towering, pretentious creations that looked more like modern art than something edible. But she wasn't going to start trading insults with the man, not at this point.

"I saw yours, too. Surprised you left the 'eight inch bangers' and 'cock au vin' off the menu. Perhaps your idea of 'love' is just too conventional for that."

"Insecure much?" she replied, and was gratified to see his color rise. *Well, you started it.*

"No. I'm just wondering if it was love that made

you make such a stupid decision.'' He shook his head. ''I can't think of any other reason for it…although that reason is baffling enough.''

''Like it's something you'd understand,'' she said, turning back to the window.

''He doesn't even know, does he?'' Phillip said, his tone colored with surprise. ''How noble. How very *sacrificing*.''

''It was my decision,'' Mari said sharply, turning to him. ''And I decided I'm not going to change what I do and what I am, just because an insecure, self-serving jackass is threatened by the man I love. No matter *what* happens.''

''So your restaurant means that little to you, then?'' Phillip said quietly.

''My restaurant means everything to me.'' Mari's voice shook, and she cursed the little sign of weakness. ''But I can live with out it if it means not giving in to you.''

''It must be nice,'' Phillip said, and she looked at him, because his voice wasn't mocking…she could've sworn he actually meant what he was saying.

''What must be nice?''

''Not to have to answer to anyone. To be that strong.'' Phillip's voice was thoughtful…then the usual sneer appeared on his face, and Mari wondered if she'd imagined the whole thing. ''Of course, giving up your restaurant for a guy you're sleeping with could be categorized as something else. Say, stupid.''

''I think you have to have a heart to understand,'' Mari said.

"Touché." Phillip shook his head. "Well. You've made your decision. You know what happens."

"If Nick wins, he can go anywhere he wants—do anything he wants," Mari said. She hated the fact that even if the restaurant could have somehow miraculously survived, there was still the possibility he would leave. Still, watching Phillip blanch was worth it. "Shutting the restaurant down isn't going to stop him…it's just going to give him no regrets when he moves on."

He scowled at her. "You're just trying to save yourself."

"You would think that," Mari said, shaking her head and walking down the hallway. "See you at the finish line, Phillip."

She walked back to the Guilty Pleasures station. All the chefs in the auditorium were now riveted to the podium. The final entries had been judged, and now the judges were meeting in a separate room and tabulating the scores.

"Hey. I was worried. You took a long time," Nick said, staring at her face. "You look pale."

She noticed he was the only one not watching for the judge's door to open. In fact, he looked cooler than anyone in the room. As if he didn't care about the outcome at all.

She thought back of what Phillip said…and what she'd responded. If they won, he'd have lots of opportunities. He would definitely be moving on.

And what will I do?

At least she could be with him, she thought. But

her heart still mourned as the fact of their competing sunk in.

I'm going to be losing the one thing I dreamed of. It was harder than she expected. She felt the stabbing pain of loss.

''I'm just waiting to see what happens,'' she finally answered him, as he put an arm around her shoulders.

''Won't be long now.''

He was right. A short, mustached judge with silver hair and bushy black eyebrows stepped up to the podium. ''We have the results,'' he said in dire tones.

The chefs held a collective breath.

''We will be reading off the rankings of the top five restaurants, then we'll post the listings of the remaining competitors,'' he said, rustling papers on the podium, either ignoring the crowd's impatience or deliberately building up the tension. Finally, he said, ''The fifth runner-up is…Henri's of Chicago, for their entry 'City in Springtime.'''

Mari barely noticed the low cheer, somewhere to her right.

''The fourth-runner up…Le Chapeau Noir of San Francisco, for 'Windows and Doorways'!''

Mari tensed at that, then grinned. Fourth place. *Wonder how he feels about that?* It was small comfort—after all, he was still top five—but the fact that he hadn't won, that they might actually *beat* him, was a small balm on her heart.

''The third-runner up…Il Fortunado from Florence, for 'Il Vesperi'! Second-runner up…Spoonful of Boston, for 'Quilt'!''

Mari closed her eyes. There was still a chance…

"And the winner of the hundred-and-fifty thousand dollar prize and the title of Champion du Internationale is…"

The words drew out, as if in slow motion.

"Reinquist's of Los Angeles, for their dynamic entry 'Midnight Garden'! Congratulations!"

There was an explosion of applause. Mari was momentarily deafened. She felt pain, and disappointment…and a strange numbness. She looked at Nick.

He, she noticed, was looking at her.

Oh, God, she thought, with a blinding flash of insight. *Not only have I lost the restaurant, I've screwed up his chances, as well. I've ruined it for both of us.*

11

Nick knew that the competition had taken its toll on Mari. Their loss had stung him as well, but at least he'd been prepared for it. Now, she was listless, and nothing he could do or say would in any way change her mind. They'd closed the restaurant for the weekend in anticipation of that Saturday challenge. Now, it was Sunday, and Mari had stayed in bed, wrapped up, seemingly unwilling to move. He'd tried comforting her, but everything he said or did didn't seem to put a dent in her depression.

"I'd just like to be alone for a little while," Mari had said instead, and even though it frustrated him, he respected her wishes.

Maybe I'll cook her something, Nick thought, pacing around his house finding restlessness catching. Then he thought about the competition, and how cooking her something special would probably remind her of it. *On second thought, maybe I'll just bring fast food and some movies.*

He sat down on his couch, at loose ends. He'd spent so much time at Mari's that this place seemed strange to him.

There was a knock on his door, and he went

to answer it. When he opened the door, his eyes widened.

"Mr. Marceau," he said, astonished. "And Mrs. Marceau."

"See, Phillip? He does still live here," Mrs. Marceau said lightly. Now Nick noticed their son behind them, standing on the steps with a look of pure venom on his face. "We've missed seeing you at the house, haven't we, Charles?"

Mr. Marceau had nodded in agreement. "Since we were in town, we thought we'd stop by and tell you ourselves—your entry was remarkable, absolutely remarkable. If you hadn't been with that group of losers, I think you would have swept the competition."

Now it was Nick's turn to frown. "They're not—"

"Never mind," Mr. Marceau said, and he made his way into the living room, his wife and Phillip following behind. Phillip was obviously loath to come in, but at his father's insistent glare, he did, remaining standing as his parents made themselves comfortable.

Nick, in sweats and a T-shirt, felt distinctly out of place.

"I have to say, this visit isn't purely social," Charles Marceau said, his voice deep and commanding. "There's some things that have been drawn to my attention…namely, you."

Phillip paced nervously, his arms crossed.

"You managed to make something from nothing, and after an internal audit, I discovered that the, ah,

allegations against you at Le Chapeau Noir were fal-
sified.''

Now Phillip turned pale. ''What is this? You said
you just wanted to see Nick!''

''See him, and show you something at the same
time,'' his father said, and now his tone turned sharp.
''You set Nick up. And once he left, you tried changing the menu. I read the financial reports, Phillip. Do
you have any idea how much business we've lost
since Nick left?''

Phillip frowned. ''The economy…''

''The economy, nothing.'' Charles's face turned
slightly reddish. ''Nick managed to turn around a little
glorified version of 'Hooters' and get it written up in
Food & Wine magazine! You've got a four-star staff
at your command, and you only get a blurb in
Saveur!''

Nick smirked at this, and Phillip glared at him.
''This is all very, um, interesting,'' Nick said. ''And
if you could clear my name and the allegations with
the rest of the culinary world, I'd appreciate it.''

''I'm going to do better than that, my boy,'' Mr.
Marceau said. ''Nick, I've wanted to offer this to you
for a long time…should've done it with Chapeau, but
that's neither here nor there. We're opening a restaurant in New York…something exotic, different, really
high-end. I want you to helm it. You can name it
whatever you want, put whatever you want on the
menu…you're the final decision maker. And the
budget will be large.''

Now Phillip turned purple. "What are you saying?"

"Son, you messed up with Chapeau by getting rid of Nick. I didn't believe you when you made your accusations, and I should've known that you'd throw away Internationale."

"We placed fourth!"

"Ha. Fourth. You should have won, and you knew it." Charles's voice was like thunder. "You'll be lucky if I even keep that high-priced restaurant of yours before I'm through. Now be quiet!"

Phillip did.

Charles nodded, as if satisfied there would be no further outbursts. "As I was saying…"

"Mr. Marceau, this is all very sudden," Nick said, his head reeling. Charles Marceau was offering to finance a restaurant for him—under his complete control. He was offering him everything he'd ever wanted or dreamed of. And Phillip's allegations were being proven wrong…while Phillip himself was possibly being put out of business. "I need time to think about it."

"I expect nothing less from you. I'm sure it'll need negotiating," Charles said, with a crafty smile. "Well, we'll leave you to think about it." He pressed his business card into Nick's hand. "Don't take too long, now."

"Um, no," Nick said.

Mrs. Marceau—Marjorie—kissed his cheek, then smiled, her face plastic-surgery tight. "We always did like you, Nick."

He turned to Phillip, seeing the pain and hatred in his eyes. Nick felt no sense of triumph at this, only a hollow twinge of pity.

''Congratulations,'' Nick said.

Phillip glowered and left. His parents followed him out the door and to the waiting limo.

Nick closed the door, and put his head against it.

Holy crap.

All he'd ever wanted. All he'd ever dreamed of.

In New York.

Away from Mari.

He shook his head. He needed to talk to her. To-night.

MARI HAD AT LAST MANAGED to get up and shower, then throw some clothes on, but that was about as productive as her day had been so far. Now, it was early evening. Nick would be here soon.

I have to figure out some way to tell him what's happened. That we'll all be looking for jobs.

Would he be angry? Of course he would be. She should have told him—it had been beyond foolish of her not to. But then what? Would he stay? Leave?

She wasn't eager to find out.

There was a knock at her door, and she walked to it, puzzled. Nick now had a key to her place. Maybe it was the crew, she thought, wincing. She'd have to tell them, too, that they'd soon be out of jobs once the restaurant closed down.

She peered through the peephole. Then she opened the door.

"Phillip Marceau. I wasn't expecting to see you so soon," she said bitterly. "Serving me with eviction papers, I assume? Or just here to gloat?"

"Not gloating. What the hell do I have to gloat about?" he asked, shaking his head.

Mari eyed him skeptically. "You mean, besides that whole fourth-place-in-Internationale thing?"

"It means less than nothing." And to her shock, he really looked like he believed that. "May I come in?"

Mari backed away and he entered her apartment.

"I suppose you know about Nick?" he asked.

She felt her heart start beating harder against her rib cage. "What about Nick?"

"My parents. They always loved him, even back when I was in school."

It suddenly struck her—there was the slightest slur in his voice. *He's drunk,* she realized. He was drunk, and he'd made his way here.

"What does that—"

He held up a hand. "The thing is, they knew he was a better chef than I was. And even though I was good with the money, good with ordering, good at *managing*…they didn't care. They wanted the *celebrity*. They wanted the *talent*." He all but spat out the words. "And they wouldn't even front me the money to open my own restaurant unless I brought Nick along as acting head chef."

Mari's eyes widened. Nick hadn't mentioned that. Maybe he hadn't known, either.

"I thought I could convince them, and I thought I was winning them over," Phillip said, in a plaintive voice. The liquor had loosened his tongue, obviously. "I wasn't. I couldn't. Nick Avery could do no wrong. So I started doing things. I refused to enter Chapeau in any competitions while he was head chef. I started arguing with him over the menu. And my parents kept taking his side."

Phillip grew red. Mari listened, fascinated.

"I knew I couldn't take it anymore. I told my parents, since Le Chapeau was doing so well, I wanted to order a second location. I thought that if I could just get away from Nick, get out of his damned shadow...I'd have a chance. And do you know what they told me?" He didn't even wait for her to answer, just looked at her with pale blue eyes full of pain. "They said it would fail if I didn't have Nick, and they weren't willing to spare him. They thought I was just a lackey who took his orders. A lackey...to *Nick*. And they favored him over their own goddamn *son*."

He looked at her, pleading. "Have you ever known what it's like," he said, his voice heartbreakingly low, "to have someone love a *restaurant* more than they love you? To think that talent and success is the only valid measure of how much they can care? What kind of humans feel that way?"

Mari sighed. "I'm sorry, Phillip," she said, and meant it.

He shrugged, and drew himself up straight. "As am I. I just wanted to let you know...I'm not going to foreclose on your restaurant. You were right at Internationale. I can't hurt him. I'll just make it easier for him to leave."

"Let's just see if you still feel that way tomorrow," Mari said. She felt bad for the guy, especially in light of what he'd just shared. But a man didn't go from Genghis Khan to Cuddles the Bunny overnight. "You're, ah, going to get home okay, right?"

"You mean the drink, I suppose," Phillip said, with a tone of injured pride. "If you're overly concerned, my driver is parked downstairs. Still, I assure you, I'm not going to be changing my mind. I'm not angry with you. And hurting you isn't going to hurt Nick anymore, anyway." He sighed. "I'm starting to believe nothing will. Especially not now. Lucky bastard."

"What do you mean?" Mari asked. Phillip was starting to walk with a dignified lurch toward the front door, but he turned back to her, his eyes light blue and full of sorrow.

"Don't you know?" he asked slowly. "Nick's taking a job. With my family. They're having him open up his own restaurant in New York, damn him."

Mari felt her heart hit her stomach and burn there.

NICK WALKED UP THE STREET to Mari's apartment, deep in thought. The restaurant, his own restaurant, the thing he'd dreamed of his whole life…or Mari, the woman he never realized he'd been waiting for his entire life.

Where did that leave him?

Would she go with me, I wonder? No, probably not, he answered himself. Her restaurant was her family. She wouldn't leave them in the lurch, unemployed. Even if he gave her the time to find them new positions, he doubted she'd want to go to New York, anyway.

In front of Mari's apartment, he paused, looking up at the rendition of her face, just across the street, on the sign. The faint naughtiness of it, the rough-sexy feel of it. And if you looked at Mari, that's what you saw—and sensed. A rough, raw, elementally sexy woman. And if you got to know her—well, then you knew her as he knew her, as a talented, imaginative chef, a sensitive soul. A wonderful friend. A wonderful *woman*.

How could he leave?

He walked up the steps slowly, then started to unlock it. She opened the door, and he caught his breath.

She was wearing her jeans, holes in the knees, her hair tumbling in rough, haphazard waves, the purple streak a rebellious match for her slumberous eyes. "I was wondering when you'd get here." She wore a T-shirt, cut short to reveal her belly-button, the sleeves removed to show her nicely toned arms. She smiled, her lower lip almost pouting in its fullness.

"Mari," he said, "we need to talk."

"Yes, we do," she said, then reached out and tugged him gently into the apartment.

The air was perfumed with something floral—jasmine, maybe, or ylang ylang, a sensual hint. It wasn't anything special—no seduction scene.

It was her scent, he noted. It was *her*.

She leaned against the couch. "So. What do you want to talk about?" Her violet eyes were clear, piercing.

"Mari," he said, his own voice rough. He reached for her, and she stepped into his arms as his mouth searched for hers, finding it with a rough urgency. "Mari," he breathed against her lips.

They made their way up the stairs to the loft. She sank down, incongruously tough-looking in the diaphanous sheets. And that was when it hit him—she portrayed her toughness for the world to see, but this was the real Mari—fragile, ethereal, full of grace.

"I love you," he murmured, and her face went from aggressively sexual to unguarded...innocent-looking, almost wary. She reached for him, and he pressed tiny kisses against her jawline, down her neck, until her breathing increased in speed. She sighed, leaning back, letting him take off her shirt with tender care. She wasn't wearing a bra beneath, and her breasts jutted forward, cream white with the deep redness of her nipples taut and erect. He could see her pulse, beating steadily in the column of her throat. He reached for her jeans, and she reached for his shirt, starting to undo the buttons securing it. He nipped at her fingertips, and she smiled...not the naughty smile, not a sexual smile. Just one of great happiness.

He let her ease the shirt off of his shoulders, and he tugged her jeans off, first one leg, then the other. She was wearing a pair of delicate pale lilac panties, edged at the top in lace. She looked at him hesitantly, and then reached for his pants. To his surprise, her fingers fumbled at the button, and he helped her, his fingers closing over hers. He let his pants drop to the floor, then closed his eyes and groaned as she ran her long fingers, trailing over the erection that bulged against the opening of his boxers, smoothing over the planes of his thighs.

He lay down next to her, feeling the warmth of her, indulging in the sweet, floral-spicy scent of her. For a moment, he just stared at her, stroking at the bangs of her hair. She let him—there was no rush, no frenzy of joining. He kissed her forehead, hearing the easy laughter at the sweetness of the gesture before she returned the favor, brushing light, ticklish kisses against his chest. He stroked every inch of her skin, tantalizing the ticklish skin behind her knees and at the V of her collarbone. He discovered she had a sweet spot just where the curve of her bottom met her thighs. In turn, she found that the delicate skin on the inside bend of his elbows sent a paroxysm of shivers running through him.

It was like sex, as well as their conversation, was something they were working around…that they wanted to enjoy every second as if it were their last, as if they might never get to explore each other's body again.

What is she thinking? Nick didn't voice the concern, merely continued in his slow, sensual exploration. *What does she feel?*

Not surprisingly, she was the one who finally nudged the intensity up, who moved against him, body to body, and pressed her skin to his, fitting herself to him until he felt like gasping.

She leaned up and kissed him. Hers were slow, drugging kisses that tasted exotic and sweet, just like her. She moved against him, until his erection emerged from his boxers, until he felt tugging fingers urging the silk out of the way. He traced a finger blindly along her panty leg, pushing the fabric aside and dipping a finger in, gratified by her small cry of pleasure. He tickled at her clitoris with one hand, then took a nipple into his mouth as she arched against him, licking at her with sure, circling strokes.

She was panting now, and her hips pushed against his hand. "Nick," she breathed, her eyes half-closed.

Now he moved in, his mouth on hers, his hunger slipping the gentle restraint he'd been floating in. Their tongues stroked against each other, twining, her full lips mobile against his insistence. She cradled his face in her hands as she dragged her nipples against his chest. It was hypnotic.

He had to be inside her. He pulled off her panties, letting them slide down her legs and tossing them aside. Now she was fully naked, her eyes smoky, filled with desire. She already had a condom out, wrapping him swiftly. She leaned up to kiss him, and he closed his eyes, allowing her to lead him to her. He felt enveloped by her—the scent of her, the silken feel of her. He sensed her fingers running down the length of him, felt his penis stroke against the satiny-softness of her thighs as she guided him closer and closer to her moist heat. He felt the tip penetrate, but she continued torturing him until finally he was poised, pressing at her. He entered with one smooth glide, and had to grit his teeth against the overwhelming pleasure of the sensation.

"Nick," she breathed again. "Oh, yes."

He carefully withdrew, half-mad by the feeling of easing out of her, and heard her whimper. Then her legs wrapped around his, pulling herself up toward him, until he was buried inside her.

"I want you," she moaned. "Forever. Please, Nick."

He couldn't verbalize how he felt—but he knew that was close to it.

He increased his tempo, feeling the smooth clenching of her muscles, feeling the way she embraced the length of him, reveling in the soft, throaty moans as he slid against her most sensitive spot. She was breathing in short, panting gasps, and he nipped at her neck until she wrapped her legs around his waist, burying him inside her.

He lost control. He increased his speed, pushing against her, losing himself to the animal side of their passion that always exploded like a conflagration when they joined like this. She was calling his name, twisting against him, and he felt the beginnings of his orgasm clutching at him.

"Mari, honey, I can't hold…" he began, but didn't have to, as she let out a keening cry. He felt the wave of wetness against him, and he knew she had found her pleasure as she shattered against him, her thighs tightening around him like a vise.

With a hoarse cry, he dove deep, plunging into her, spilling himself into her before collapsing against the bed, barely able to keep himself from crushing her completely.

They stayed like that for a moment, quiet, just the scent of their lovemaking and the sheen of their sweat between them, their hearts beating in time.

How can I leave?

Before he could speak, she did.

"You're leaving." It wasn't a question. "I know that."

He closed his eyes.

She had a hell of a sense of timing.

"I haven't decided yet," he said, leaning to one side. They were face to face, companionably naked. "How did you know…that it was an option, I mean?"

She shrugged. "Phillip stopped by."

"Phillip Marceau was here? What did he want?" He'd written Phillip off…the man had looked absolutely destroyed when he'd left with his parents. Was Phillip trying one last effort to sabotage him, by trying to turn Mari against him? What else could he do?

"He said that you were going to accept his parents' offer. That you were opening a restaurant in New York."

Nick studied her. "And you believed him? You believed I'd take an offer like that without talking to you first?"

She propped herself up on one elbow, her hair looking wild, her face looking vulnerable. Her eyes were wide and clear. "Nick, I love you. And I believe that you…love me," she said, her voice choked. "And I don't think that you'd leave without talking to me first."

"Well, I'm glad you realize that," Nick said, with a sigh.

"But…I still think that you'll leave."

Nick sat up. "I said, I hadn't decided yet," he said, hating the fact that his voice sounded so defensive.

"You're not sure?" she asked quietly. "It could go either way, then?"

Nick sighed, heavily. "I don't have to get back to them right away."

"I'd say you should take it."

He shook his head. "I know you want what's best for me…"

"No," she corrected, and it was as if she were suddenly clothed—all the vulnerability and fragileness he'd noted before, when he'd taken her to bed, became cloaked by her change in expression. It was the toughness, he realized. And it wasn't an act. "I want what's best for *me.*"

He looked at her, not comprehending.

She stroked his face, studying him, smiling… crying. She was staring at him, like she was staring into his soul.

"If you stay without finding out what would happen if you opened your own restaurant, you'll hate me. I don't want that. And I very nearly…" She took a deep breath. "I know what it's like to lose your dream, Nick. I won't do that to you."

"Then come with me," he said, kissing her. "Work with me, live with me."

"No," she said, and it was like a hammer hitting

his chest. "I won't give up my dream, either. I came too close to losing it already."

He leaned up on one arm. "So...where does that leave us?"

She shook her head.

"That's the problem," she said in a soft voice. "It...doesn't."

He stared at her. "That's it, then? You just want me to leave?"

"Nick, you won't be happy if you stay. Find out. If it's supposed to work out, it will."

"That is such *crap!*" he said, jumping up. "I'm just supposed to go to New York without you?"

"Tell me something," Mari said sharply, her eyes ablaze. "If I weren't in the picture, would you go to New York to open your own restaurant?"

"In a heartbeat," he said without hesitation, then closed his eyes. "But you *are* in the picture," he amended.

"Yes, I know," she said with a slow, sad smile. "But even with me in it...did you consider it anyway?"

He looked down at the coverlet, and then reluctantly nodded.

She stood up, all naked splendor and comforting, quiet love. "Pack warm," she said, before turning and heading for the bathroom. "Fall's coming and it...gets cold...in New York."

He heard the bathroom door close, and realized that that was it. His sojourn at Guilty Pleasures was over.

12

"READY ON EIGHT?" Mari called out, looking at Tiny. "I've got the Hot Chicks and the Cock au Vin tanning under the lamps, Tiny, where are my steaks?"

"Ready on eight," Tiny said, slightly out of breath. He slammed the oven shut with his hip, and both he and Mari slid their plates out onto the order window. A perky redheaded waitress—new to the staff—picked up with the help of Mo.

"Damn, feel like my arm's gonna fall off," Paulo grumbled from the sauté station. Zooey was expediting, her high, clear soprano getting a little hoarse around the edges. "I thought that us tanking at the contest was going to screw us up. I think we're busier than ever."

"I know we're busier than ever," Mari said, focusing with all the precision of a surgeon at the sauté station. She was helping Paulo...but it looked like Tiny was falling behind. She'd give him a hand in a minute.

Lindsay stepped out of the back room. She was wearing jeans and a long-sleeved T-shirt. She had been helping out on the night shift, although making salads and plating desserts was about the extent of her culinary achievements. "Good news," she said, excited. "We did about five hundred dinners last night!"

There was a ragged cheer, then a groan as more duplicates printed out on their new order machine. Zooey picked them up and continued calling out the orders.

"Looks like six hundred tonight," Paulo groaned.

Mari should have been tired—and probably was, if she thought about it. The trick, she learned, was *not* to think about it.

Wonder what he's doing right now.

She picked up a pot, then hissed as she scalded her wrist. She put it down with a clatter.

Not going to think about Nick Avery. No time for it, no point to it.

"Lindsay, you doing salads tonight?" she said instead.

"Sorry," Lindsay apologized, going back to the station. She tossed together the candied pecans, fresh pears and gorgonzola cheese, then drizzled the balsamic vinagrette over everything. "Five up. Fire it."

Mari moved into action. Two more steaks, three more salads. She helped Zooey with some desserts.

She was numb. She'd been numb for the past month.

Out of curiosity, she'd driven past Nick's place a week ago. The apartment now had a silver minivan in its short, steep driveway. Nick must have put his stuff in storage, more than likely, or had professionals move him to New York. If the Marceaus were bank-rolling him, she would imagine that he'd go in style.

And in San Francisco's crazed housing shortage, no apartment was vacant for long.

She didn't let it hurt. She just let it…sink in.

She kept working. She spent every waking moment in the restaurant or at the markets. Her life was inundated with the scents of cooking food, with the hellish heat of the kitchen, with the jostling of bodies and the fluttering of dupe sheets on the order board. She didn't know what miracle had gotten them so busy, but she thanked it nonetheless—not just for the financial sake of her business, but from the sheer fact that as long as she was moving, she wasn't hurting.

At least, not as much.

When midnight finally hit, the crew was groaning like injured athletes. They cleaned slowly. For most of them, it was because they were feeling the screaming soreness of muscles. For Mari, it was because she knew that when she locked up, she'd be heading to Tiger if she was lucky, though not many of the crew had the energy anymore. Certainly not after their latest barrage. Instead, more than likely, it would mean that she would go back to her empty loft, crawl into the bed, and fight against falling asleep by watching countless television shows that she'd never remember. Then dreams of Nick would come…actually, nightmares of Nick. The worst one had come late at night, when she'd dreamed that Nick had spent the day with her. They'd shopped at the farmer's market, cooked and joked together and with her crew. Then he'd spend the night in her house, fooling around in the kitchen, snuggling up beside her in bed.

When she'd woken to the cool pillow beside her, she wept into it.

"Mari?" Kyla stepped into the kitchen. "There's a party of people that doesn't want to leave."

Mari rolled her eyes. Even though she didn't want to go home, she didn't necessarily want to stay for a rowdy, possibly tanked bunch of partiers. "Can't Rob handle it?" Mari said, referring to their new bartender.

Kyla shook her head. "They want to talk to you, I think."

Tiny stepped behind her, as did Paulo. Mari sighed. "Guess I'll go take care of them, then," she said, and they all walked out.

There was a table of twelve people, with the remnants of an obviously large meal in front of them. There were also several bottles of wine, empty, littering the table. Three of them were singing, slightly off-key. The others were joking, telling some story that involved wild gesticulations, and there was a great deal of laughter all around. When she stepped up to them, she couldn't help noticing that several of them looked familiar.

"I'm Mari Salazar, the owner here," she said, hoping to keep things pleasant as she bounced the group. "Was everything satisfactory?"

"You rock, girl." One balding man, on the portly side, lifted his glass.

Mari smiled. "Well, thanks. Unfortunately, gentlemen, we have to close...."

"You showed 'em," a short, dark-haired, dark-eyed man said with a grin. "You showed 'em all."

She stopped. "Showed who what?"

Finally, a tall, razor-thin man with scarred hands and tattoos on his shoulder stood up. "A toast, to Mari Salazar," he said. "The only chef at Internationale with the guts to cook real food."

Mari blinked as the men stood up, raising their glasses and cheering her in a variety of languages. She squinted at the tall man. "You were there. You were competing with…"

"Stars," he said, with a smile. "Sous-chef. Head chef there is a boot-licker, you don't need to tell any-body I said that, but just so you know. And you didn't even care that day—you still helped us when we were in a disaster."

"I'm from Strazzi's," the dark man said. "Don't suppose I can steal that recipe for the chicken, huh? Almost set my mouth on fire." He grinned. "Just the way I like it."

There were several other compliments. The men ranged from sous-chefs to dishwashers, and they'd all come here…to try her food. And to show their sup-port.

Mari felt her eyes welling up with tears as she smiled, and nodded to them. She turned to the bar-tender. "Set 'em up with a round. On me."

The bartender, openly grinning, nodded. Mari and the crew retreated to the kitchen.

"We're going to make it, aren't we?" Zooey said, with a quiet tone of pride.

Mari thought about it, then thought about Nick, try-ing so desperately to get the recognition he'd been chasing ever since his Culinary School days. She thought about her own need—thought about herself.

She gave Zooey a half hug, wiping at her eyes with the back of her hand. "Yeah," she said, slowly. "Yeah, we're going to make it."

NICK STOOD IN HIS KITCHEN. *His* kitchen, the future site of his restaurant. Le Chapeau Noir had been swank, he thought—this was downright *decadent*. Sub-zero freezers, top-of-the-line ranges, a wine cellar that would make most collectors weep. And Charles Marceau had assured him that he could order the best, most expensive ingredients-white truffle oil, Normandy butter, Scharfenberger chocolate, dry-aged filet mignon. He was like a kid loose in a candy store, and every waking moment had been channeled into developing the décor, the menu, the way everything would work. He was exactly where he'd always wanted to be.

So why can't you stop thinking about Mari?

Mr. Marceau stepped in. "Everything satisfactory, Nick?"

Nick nodded. "Yes. I couldn't ask for more." He couldn't ask for anything else that the man could provide, anyway.

"I figure, six months, and we'll be up and running. I've got chefs from some of my other restaurants vying for the position, and we'll have a contest—survival of the fittest, as it were." Charles laughed, a brittle sounding noise. "You'll only get the best, Nick, that's a guarantee. I want your restaurant to be *the* place to go in Manhattan.''

Nick nodded absently.

"I'll also suggest you taking on Dan Patterson as your general manager,'' Charles said, clapping a hand on Nick's shoulder. Nick felt the urge to shrug it off, but knew it would look impolite, so he tried as best he could to seem interested. "You ever want to know what's going on politically in your kitchen—what sous-chef is bucking for your job, what line chef is drinking too much, what prep cook is stealing from the walk-in—Dan's your man.''

Mari never worried about stuff like that—the political stuff, he thought. The crew would have cut off their left hands before taking anything from her. In fact, he wouldn't be surprised if Paulo actually snuck ingredients *into* the pantry.

He missed her crew, too, he realized. Tiny's staunch loyalty, Paulo's lightning-quick humor, Zooey's naiveté were hard to forget. But most of all, he missed Mari.

"You're going to be the talk of the town, Nick my boy. You're going to be famous,'' Charles said, and Nick could see in his face that he had already envisioned everything that was certain to follow. "You're going to be a *star*.''

Nick thought about it. His face on the cover of magazines? Maybe on television? Women fawning over him, chefs cowering? Phillip, sneering in some second-rate venue in Omaha, eating his heart out?

What the hell did I want all that for?

He looked at Charles, and saw for the first time that the man wasn't looking to showcase Nick—he was looking for glory, and saw Nick as his ticket. He saw Nick as a money-maker.

He didn't see Nick as a star.

He saw Nick as a *tool*.

I. Am. So. Stupid.

Nick shook his head. "I can't do this."

Charles was too deep in his monologue to notice Nick shrugging his hand off. "I'm telling you, this is only the beginning. I knew that Phillip couldn't handle a project like this—that's why I held back on the reins for Le Chapeau Noir. I knew that he didn't have the talent or the vision…"

"I said, I can't do it," Nick said, a little more emphatically.

"Of course you can," Charles said, brushing Nick's statement away like an annoying fly. "Why do you think I insisted that Phillip have you as head chef before I set him up with the restaurant in the first place?"

Nick stared at him, aghast. "You *what?*"

"And you took up the slack. That's why I always went to you when I wanted something done. Phillip's my son…but business is business." He chuckled, and the sound turned Nick's stomach. "You understand that. That's why you're the right man for the job."

Nick leaned back against the cold metal of the countertop.

That's why Phillip hated me. It was so obvious, and he'd been so very, very dumb.

He realized he had nothing else to prove. He'd get everything he thought he wanted and nothing that he needed—and he'd lose his soul daily as Charles molded him into a little wanna-be Marceau. Where the only thing more important than the food was the bottom line.

"I am not saying that I can't handle it," Nick corrected. "I'm saying that I won't do it. I made a mistake accepting this job. I thought I had something to show everyone. I don't. Not to people like you. Not to myself."

"Wait a minute," Charles stared at him like he was speaking another language. "You're *quitting?*"

Nick nodded.

"I can't imagine anyone else could offer you as impressive a deal as this, Nick," he started coldly. "Has someone else.."

"No, it's not like that." Nick paused. "Well, I suppose you could say that I am going to work for a competitor. But not in New York. I'm going back to San Francisco. I never should have left."

"You and I made a deal," Charles said, his voice low and harsh. "You renege, and I'll see to it that it gets *very* difficult—no, *impossible*—to work anywhere again. I don't care what they're offering you."

"What they're offering me is loyalty," Nick said, pleased by the way the man's face turned baffled. "And love. And family."

Slowly, Charles blinked. "You're going back to that *hole-in-the-wall?* That…that pornographic Denny's, for pity's sake?"

Nick nodded.

Charles laughed. "I won't have to ruin you. You're doing the job for me. You'd be willing to walk away from your own restaurant—from more money than you've probably made in your entire life—all for…" He blinked, realizing he didn't have a conclusion for that sentence. "All for what?"

"If you have to ask," Nick said, turning, "then I can't explain it to you."

TWO-THIRTY. MARI GLANCED at the clock. She'd been working from eight-thirty in the morning to midnight, and now for the past two and a half hours, she was working on a chocolate bread pudding with a pecan strudel topping. Maybe…she was working on variations of both. And she had three small batches, made from some of the little bit of stale bread that was left at the restaurant. She might even experiment with made-from-scratch brownies.

Say what you will about insomnia, Mari thought, at least it makes me productive. She'd probably create at least four more dishes before the hallucinations started to kick in.

She leaned back against her fridge, closing her eyes for a second.

She couldn't go on like this. That much was obvious.

Would it be such a hardship? New York was a beautiful place. They needed all the good chefs they could get. And they had seasons, she remembered. Maybe she'd like fall.

You'd probably hate winter.

Well, okay, there was that. But she'd have Nick to keep her warm, and that was what was important, wasn't it? He'd probably even hire her…turnabout was fair play.

And what would everybody on the crew do?

They were all talented—they could get jobs easily. Was she really worried about them, or was she using them as an excuse not to take that final risk?

She loved them. She loved their spirit. And she loved her restaurant.

This was the choice Nick had to make—the one you pushed, she reminded herself. She'd just have to learn to live with it…or die trying.

"You're burning your…what is that, anyway?"

She didn't open her eyes. "It's bread pudding." She sighed. "Okay, okay, I'll get it."

She was so used to sensing Nick, the fact that her overtired subconscious had created Nick's voice so perfectly was no surprise. She pulled the bread pudding out from the oven, then turned.

The *vision* of him, however, was something of a shock.

She dropped the pan.

"Careful," he said, grabbing a second pair of oven mitts and cleaning up the mess. He looked just as she remembered. Okay, a little more rumpled than she remembered. And tired—he looked tired, especially around the eyes. He had a rough days growth of beard, and he was eyeing her like a dessert he wanted to sample.

"Obviously I've hit the wall," she said, as she watched him rescue her other dessert attempts, leaving them on the butcher-block counter to cool. She shut the oven off with a click. "Normally I'm in bed before I see you this clearly."

"I can't believe you didn't hear me come in."

She blinked. Then she walked up to him, her fingers reaching forward.

She pinched his shoulder. Hard.

"Ouch! Dammit," he grimaced. "What was that for?"

She smiled. "You're…really here," she said softly.

She threw herself into his arms.

"I used my key," he said. "I didn't give it back. I was praying you didn't change the locks."

"Didn't think I'd need to," she said. "Didn't think you'd come back."

He held her against him. She could hear his heart beating strong if somewhat unsteadily under her ear. She pressed as tightly as she could to him, relishing the feel of him kissing her temples, stroking her back. "I wasn't ready. I'm sorry."

She pulled back enough to look at him. "Are you back…for a visit?" She didn't want to ask directly, but her heart was in her eyes.

"Not exactly." He stroked her cheek, then kissed her gently on the lips. "As it happens, I need a job."

She stared at him. "You gave up the restaurant?"

He shrugged. "I figured out it wasn't really what I wanted, after all." He hugged her to him, and she smiled. "I worked it out that I didn't want to be financed by a rich man who thought that being successful and prominent was more important than being a good father. And I didn't want a bunch of backstabbing chefs that I'd need daily reports on. And I certainly didn't want to be written up in a bunch of magazines and idolized by a bunch of people who really didn't matter to me, when I could be here, among people who are my friends…and loved by the woman I love most.''

She kissed him long and hard, with all the passion she'd stored up since he went away.

"I love you," she said. "I love you so much."

"I love you, too," he said.

She hugged him tight.

"Besides," he whispered, starting to tug off her shirt. "If I stay here, I can still make all the menus myself, anyway."

She looked into his eyes, with a mix of passion and longing.

"Like hell," she said, and while he was laughing she kissed him.

Epilogue

Five Months Later

CHAOS REIGNED in the Guilty Pleasures kitchen. And they'd only opened their door an hour ago. Nick looked around. Leon was there, helping train the new line cooks who'd been hired. Lindsay was studying Leon's advice diligently—she had decided to become more useful in the kitchen, and with her usual drive, she'd been practicing for the past two months. Mo was busily taking reservations for the week, smiling as he filled the book and told people there wasn't room— they'd been doing such gangbuster business, there were lines down the block every night. Tiny, Zooey, Juan and Paulo were discussing the menu for a competition they were thinking of entering in a few months. All in all, the place was a noisy, riotous, busy conflagration.

Nick grinned. It felt like he'd come home.

He noticed arms around his waist, and turned to see Mari smiling up at him. ''How's it going?'' she murmured, kissing him.

He smiled, his arms going around hers as well. ''We're going to get slammed tonight,'' he said, ''and the line cooks are coming along.''

"Great," she said, tugging him toward the back room and away from the noise of the kitchen. "If we're going to expand into more of the building, then we're going to need all the help we can get."

Nick shook his head. "I still can't believe Phillip's agreeing to lease us more of the building, and help kick in on the renovation."

Mari smiled, stroking his cheek. "It's different now. Since you came back, there isn't any rivalry."

He shrugged. "Since he shut down Le Chapeau Noir, too," he said. It still felt weird. He wasn't ready to trust Phillip completely yet, but it was nice to see a glimpse of the man he'd been friends with back in school.

He leaned against the desk, pulling Mari against him. "I never thought I'd be this happy," he said, kissing her neck and smiling at the little breathless gasp she made. His hands cupped her backside.

"Door," she said, tugging away and shutting the door they'd only had installed in the past month. She clicked the lock in place, and then looked at him, her eyes hungry. "Sorry. What were you saying?"

She stepped between his legs, brushing against him, her breasts teasing his chest.

"I was saying," he resumed, stroking the under-sides of her breasts, smoothing his hands down her sides to her hips, "that I never thought I'd be this happy."

She looked into his eyes, and his hands stopped roaming for a minute. "After I lost my restaurant— my *first* restaurant—I thought I'd lost everything that mattered to me," she whispered. "But if I hadn't lost all that, I never would have found you."

"That's it exactly," he whispered, then kissed her roughly, enjoying the feel of her hands in his hair, the way her tongue rubbed against his. "I love you."

She smiled. "I..."

There was a banging on the door, and the two of them turned.

"Hey, lunch hour is coming up," Paulo said, humor obvious in his tone. "You two aren't going to be long in your *meeting,* are you?"

Nick looked at Mari, with a slow, seductive smile. "Are we going to be long?" he whispered.

She reached for his pants, grinning back impishly. "We'll be out in a minute," she yelled back.

He could hear the whole crew laugh in the other room, and heard Paulo's derisive snort.

"Aw," he said, before Nick heard him turn away, "you two say that every day."

"I think they're onto us," Nick said, tugging at Mari's shirt.

"Shut up," she replied, her eyes glowing, "and kiss me. We have to hurry up and get back to work."

Modern Romance™
...seduction and
passion guaranteed

Tender Romance™
...love affairs that
last a lifetime

Medical Romance™
...medical drama
on the pulse

Historical Romance™
...rich, vivid and
passionate

Sensual Romance™
...sassy, sexy and
seductive

Blaze Romance™
...the temperature's
rising

27 new titles every month.

Live the emotion

MILLS & BOON®

MB3

Next month don't miss –

PASSION IN PARADISE

*As the temperature rises and pulses race
faster, three couples surrender to the
heated seduction of an island
in paradise…*

On sale 5th March 2004

*Available at most branches of WHSmith, Tesco, Martins,
Borders, Eason, Sainsbury's and all good paperback bookshops.*

0204/05

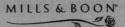

FREE!

2 Books
and a surprise gift!

We would like to take this opportunity to thank you for reading this Mills & Boon® book by offering you the chance to take TWO more specially selected titles, one from the Blaze Romance™ series and one from the Sensual Romance™ series absolutely FREE! We're also making this offer to introduce you to the benefits of the Reader Service™ —

- ★ FREE home delivery
- ★ FREE gifts and competitions
- ★ FREE monthly Newsletter
- ★ Books available before they're in the shops
- ★ Exclusive Reader Service discount

Accepting these FREE books and gift places you under no obligation to buy; you may cancel at any time, even after receiving your free shipment. Simply complete your details below and return the entire page to the address below. **You don't even need a stamp!**

YES! Please send me 2 free Romance books and a surprise gift. I understand that unless you hear from me, I will receive 4 superb new titles every month for just £11.18 (2 Blaze and 2 Sensual), postage and packing free. I am under no obligation to purchase any books and may cancel my subscription at any time. The free books and gift will be mine to keep in any case.

K4ZEE

Ms/Mrs/Miss/Mr ....Initials ....
BLOCK CAPITALS PLEASE

Surname ....

Address ....

....

....Postcode ....

Send this whole page to:
UK: The Reader Service, FREEPOST CN81, Croydon, CR9 3WZ
EIRE: The Reader Service, PO Box 4546, Kilcock, County Kildare (stamp required)

Offer not valid to current Reader Service subscribers to this series. We reserve the right to refuse an application and applicants must be aged 18 years or over. Only one application per household. Terms and prices subject to change without notice. Offer expires 30th May 2004. As a result of this application, you may receive offers from Harlequin Mills & Boon and other carefully selected companies. If you would prefer not to share in this opportunity please write to The Data Manager at the address above.

Mills & Boon® is a registered trademark owned by Harlequin Mills & Boon Limited.
Sensual Romance™ & Blaze Romance™ are being used as a trademarks.
The Reader Service™ is being used as a trademark.